W9-AHH-212

A McKettrick Christmas

Center Point
Large Print

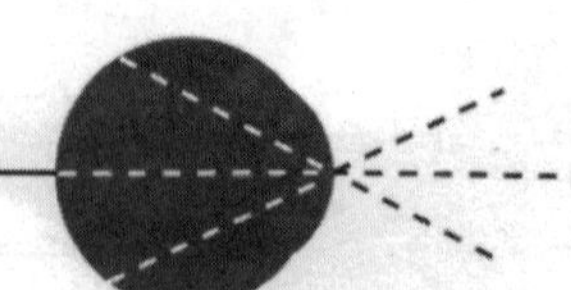

This Large Print Book carries the
Seal of Approval of N.A.V.H.

A McKettrick Christmas

LINDA LAEL MILLER

CENTER POINT PUBLISHING
THORNDIKE, MAINE

This Center Point Large Print edition
is published in the year 2008 by arrangement with
Harlequin Books, S.A.

The text of this Large Print edition is unabridged.
In other aspects, this book may vary
from the original edition.
Printed in the United States of America.
Set in 16-point Times New Roman type.

ISBN: 978-1-60285-323-2

Library of Congress Cataloging-in-Publication Data

Miller, Linda Lael.
A McKettrick Christmas / Linda Lael Miller.
p. cm.
ISBN 978-1-60285-323-2 (library binding : alk. paper)
1. Texas--Fiction. 2. Christmas stories. 3. Large type books. I. Title.

PS3563.I41373M53 2008
813'.54--dc22

2008038474

Dear Reader,

It's a pleasure to revisit one of my all-time favorite families, the McKettricks, and find Holt's daughter, Lizzie, all grown up and convinced she's in love with the wrong man, while the *right* one is practically at her elbow! Like all the McKettricks, Lizzie's pretty sure of her opinions, but she's in for some surprises.

I also wanted to write today to tell you about a special group of people with whom I've recently become involved. It is The Humane Society of the United States (HSUS), specifically their Pets for Life program.

The Pets for Life program is one of the best ways to help your local shelter: that is to help keep animals out of shelters in the first place. Something as basic as keeping a collar and tag on your pet all the time, so if he gets out and gets lost, he can be returned home. Being a responsible pet owner. Spaying or neutering your pet. And not giving up when things don't go perfectly. If your dog digs in the yard, or your cat scratches the furniture, know that these are problems that can be addressed. You can find all the information about these problems—and many other common ones—at www.petsforlife.org. This campaign is focused on keeping pets and their people together for a lifetime.

As many of you know, my own household includes two dogs, two cats and four horses, so this is a cause that is near and dear to my heart. I hope you'll get involved along with me.

May you be blessed.
With love,

Linda Lael Miller

For all those people, everywhere,
who make a loving space for pets
in their hearts and their homes.

A McKettrick Christmas

Chapter One

December 22, 1896

Lizzie McKettrick leaned slightly forward in her seat, as if to do so would make the train go faster. Home. She was going *home,* at long last, to the Triple M Ranch, to her large, rowdy family. After more than two years away, first attending Miss Ridgely's Institute of Deportment and Refinement for Young Women, then normal school, Lizzie was returning to the place and the people she loved—for good. She would arrive a day before she was expected, too, and surprise them all—her papa, her stepmother, Lorelei, her little brothers, John Henry, Gabriel, and Doss. She had presents for everyone, most sent ahead from San Francisco weeks ago, but a few especially precious ones secreted away in one of her three huge travel trunks.

Only her grandfather, Angus McKettrick, the patriarch of the sprawling clan, knew she'd be there that very evening. He'd be waiting, Lizzie thought happily, at the small train station in Indian Rock, probably at the reins of one of the big flat-bed sleighs used to carry feed to snowbound cattle on the range. She'd warned him, in her most recent letter, that she'd be bringing all her belongings with her, for this homecoming was permanent—not just a brief visit, like the last couple of Christmases.

Lizzie smiled a mischievous little smile. Even Angus, her closest confidant except for her parents, didn't know *all* the facts.

She glanced sideways at Whitley Carson, slumped against the sooty window in the seat next to hers, huddled under a blanket, sound asleep. His breath fogged the glass, and every so often, he stirred fitfully, grumbled something.

Alas, for all his sundry charms, Whitley was not an enthusiastic traveler. His complaints, over the three days since they'd boarded the first train in San Francisco, had been numerous.

The train was filthy.

There was no dining car.

The cigar smoke roiling overhead made him cough.

He was never going to be warm again.

And *what* in God's green earth had possessed the woman three rows behind them to undertake a journey of any significant distance with two rascally children and a fussy infant in tow?

Now the baby let out a pitiable squall.

Lizzie, used to babies because there were so many on the Triple M, was unruffled. Whitley's obvious annoyance troubled her. Although she planned to teach, married or not, she hoped for a houseful of children of her own someday—healthy, noisy, rambunctious ones, raised to be confident adults and freethinkers.

It was hard, in the moment, to square the Whitley

she was seeing now with the kind of father she had hoped he would be.

The man across the aisle from her laid down his newspaper, stood and stretched. He'd boarded the train several hours earlier, in Phoenix, carrying what looked like a doctor's bag, its leather sides cracked and scratched. His waistcoat was clean but threadbare, and he wore neither a hat nor a sidearm—the absence of both unusual in the still-wild Arizona Territory.

Although Lizzie expected Whitley to propose marriage once they were home with her family, she'd been stealing glances at the stranger ever since he entered the railroad car. There was something about him, beyond his patrician good looks, that constantly drew her attention.

His hair was dark, and rather too long, his eyes brown and intense, bespeaking formidable intelligence. Although he probably wasn't a great deal older than Lizzie, who would turn twenty on her next birthday, there was a maturity in his manner and countenance that intrigued her. It was as though he'd lived many other lives, in other times and places, and extracted wisdom from them all.

She heard him speak quietly to the harried mother, turned and felt a peculiar little clench in the secret regions of her heart when she saw him holding the child, bundled in a shabby patchwork quilt coming apart at the seams.

Whitley slumbered on, oblivious.

There were few other passengers in the car. A wan and painfully thin soldier in a blue army uniform, recuperating from some dire illness or injury, by the looks of him. A portly salesman who held what must have been his sample case on his lap, one hand clasping the handle, the other a smoldering cigar. He seemed to have an inexhaustible supply of the things, and he'd been puffing on them right along. An older couple, gray-haired and companionable, though they seldom spoke, accompanied by an exotic white bird in a splendid brass cage. Glorious blue feathers adorned its head, and when the cage wasn't covered in its red velvet drape, the bird chattered.

All of them, except for Whitley, of course, were strangers. And seeing Whitley in this new and disconcerting light made *him* seem like a stranger, too.

A fresh wave of homesickness washed over Lizzie. She longed to be among people she knew. Lorelei, her stepmother, would be baking incessantly these days, hiding packages and keeping secrets. Her father, Holt, would be locked away in his wood shop between ranch chores, building sleds and toy buckboards and dollhouses, some of which would be gifts to Lizzie's brothers and various cousins, though the majority were sure to find their way onto some of the poorer homesteads surrounding the Triple M.

There were always a lot of presents tucked into the branches of the family's tree and piled beneath it, and an abundance of savory food, too, but a McKettrick Christmas centered on giving to folks who didn't have so much. Lorelei, Lizzie herself, and all the aunts made rag dolls and cloth animals with stuffing inside, to be distributed at the community celebration at the church on Christmas Eve.

The stranger walked the aisle with the baby, bringing Lizzie's mind back to the here and now. He glanced down into her upturned face as he passed. He didn't actually smile—as little as she knew about him, she *had* figured out that he was both solemn and taciturn by nature—but something moved in his eyes.

Lizzie felt a flash of shame. *She* should have offered to spell the anxious mother three rows back. Already the child was settling down a little, cooing and drooling on the man's once-white shirt. If he minded that, he gave no indication of it.

Beyond the train windows, heavy flakes of snow swirled in the gathering twilight, and while Lizzie willed the train to pick up speed, it seemed to be slowing down instead.

She was just about to speak to the man, reach out for the baby, when a horrific roar, like a thousand separate thunderheads suddenly clashing together, erupted from every direction and from no direction at all. The car jerked violently, stopped with a shudder fit to fling the entire train off the tracks, tilted wildly to one side, then came right again with a sickening jolt.

The bird squawked in terror, wings making a frantic slapping sound.

Lizzie, nearly thrown from her seat, felt the clasp of a firm hand on her shoulder, looked up to see the stranger, still upright, the baby safe in the curve of his right arm. He'd managed somehow to stay on his feet, retain his hold on the child *and* keep Lizzie from slamming into the seat in front of her.

"Wh-what . . . ?" she murmured, bewildered by shock.

"An avalanche, probably," the man replied calmly, as though a massive snowslide was no more than he would have expected of a train ride through the rugged high country of the northern Arizona Territory.

Whitley, shaken awake, was as frightened as the bird. "Are we derailed?" he demanded.

The stranger ignored him. "Is anyone hurt?" he asked, of the company in general, patting the baby's back and bouncing it a little against his shoulder.

"My arm," the woman in back whimpered. "My arm—"

"Nobody panic," the man in the aisle said, shoving the baby into Lizzie's arms and turning to take the medical kit from the rack above his seat. He spoke quietly to the elderly couple; Lizzie saw them nod their heads. They were all right, then.

"Nobody panic!" the bird cawed. "Nobody panic!"

Despite the gravity of the situation, Lizzie had to smile at that.

Whitley rubbed his neck, eyeing the medical bag, after tossing a brief, disgruntled glare at the bird. "I think I'm hurt," he said. "You're a doctor, aren't you? I need laudanum."

"Laudanum!" the bird demanded.

"Hush, Woodrow," the old lady said. Her husband put the velvet drapery in place, covering the cage, and Woodrow quieted instantly.

The doctor's answer to Whitley was a clipped nod and, "Yes, I'm a physician. My name is Morgan Shane. I'll look you over once I've seen to Mrs. Halifax's arm."

The baby began to shriek in Lizzie's embrace, straining for its mother.

"Make him shut up," Whitley said. "I'm in pain."

"Shut up!" Woodrow mimicked, his call muted by the drapery. "I'm in pain!"

Lizzie paid Whitley no mind, got to her feet. "Dr. Shane?"

He was crouched in the aisle now, next to the baby's mother, gently examining her right arm. "Yes?" he said, a little snappishly, not looking away from what he was doing. The older children, a boy and a girl, huddled together in the inside seat, clinging to each other.

"The baby—the way he's crying—do you think he could be injured?"

"My baby is a girl," the woman said, between groans.

"She's just had a bad scare," Dr. Shane told Lizzie, speaking more charitably this time. "Like the rest of us."

"I think we's buried," the soldier exclaimed.

"Buried!" Woodrow agreed, with a rustle of feathers.

Sure enough, solid snow, laced with tree branches, dislodged stones and other debris, pressed against all the windows on one side of the car. On the other, Lizzie knew from previous journeys aboard the same train, a steep grade plummeted deep into the red rocks of the valley below.

"Just a bad sprain," Dr. Shane told Mrs. Halifax matter-of-factly. "I'll make you a sling, and if the pain gets to be too bad, I can give you a little medicine, but I'd rather not. You're nursing the baby, aren't you?"

Mrs. Halifax nodded, biting her lower lip. Lizzie realized with a start that the woman was probably close to her own age, perhaps even a year or two younger. She was thin to the point of emaciation, and her clothes were worn, faded from much washing, and although the children wore coats, frayed at the cuffs and hems and long since outgrown, she had none.

Lizzie thought with chagrin of the contents of her trunks. Woolen dresses. Shawls. The warm black coat with the royal blue velvet collar Lorelei had sent in honor of her graduation from normal school, so she'd be both comfortable and stylish on the trip home. She'd elected to save the costly garment for Sunday best.

She went back up the aisle, still carrying the baby,

to where Whitley sat. "We need that blanket," she said.

Whitley scowled and hunched deeper into the soft folds. "I'm *injured,*" he said. "I could be in shock."

Exasperated, Lizzie tapped one foot. "You are *not* injured," she replied. "But Mrs. Halifax is. Whitley, *give me that blanket.*"

Whitley only tightened his two-handed grasp, so that his knuckles went white, and shook his head stubbornly, and in that moment of stark and painful clarity, Lizzie knew she'd never marry Whitley Carson. Not even if he begged on bended knee, which was not very likely, but a satisfying fantasy, nonetheless.

"Here's mine, ma'am," the soldier called out from the back, offering a faded quilt ferreted from his oversize haversack.

The peddler, his cigar apparently snubbed out during the crash, but still in his mouth, opened his sample case. "I've got some dish towels, here," he told Dr. Shane. "Finest Egyptian cotton, handwoven. One of them ought to do for a sling."

The doctor nodded, thanked the peddler, took the quilt from the soldier.

"If I could just get to my trunks," Lizzie fretted, settling the slightly quieter baby girl on a practiced hip. Between her younger brothers and her numerous cousins, she'd had a lot of practice looking after small children.

Dr. Shane, in the process of fashioning the fine

Egyptian dish towel into a sling for Mrs. Halifax's arm, favored her with a disgusted glance. "This is no time to be worrying about your wardrobe," he said.

Stung, Lizzie flushed. She opened her mouth to explain why she wanted access to her baggage—for truly altruistic reasons—but pride stopped her.

"I'm in pain here!" Whitley complained, from the front of the car.

"I'm in pain here," Woodrow muttered, but he was settling down.

"Perhaps you should see to your husband," Dr. Shane said tersely, leveling a look at Lizzie as he straightened in the aisle.

More heat suffused Lizzie's cheeks. It was cold now, and getting colder; she could see her breath. "Whitley Carson," she said, "is most certainly *not* my husband."

A semblance of a smile danced in Dr. Shane's dark eyes, but never quite touched his mouth. "Well, then," he drawled, "you have more sense than I would have given you credit for, Miss . . . ?"

"McKettrick," Lizzie said, begrudging him even her name, but unable to stop herself from giving it, just the same. "Lizzie McKettrick."

About to turn to the soldier, who might or might not have been hurt, Dr. Shane paused, raised his eyebrows. He recognized the McKettrick name, she realized. He was bound for Indian Rock, the last stop on the route, or he would not have been on that particular train, and he might even have some business with her family.

A horrible thought struck her. Was someone sick? Her papa? Lorelei? Her grandfather? During her time away from home, letters had flown back and forth—Lizzie corresponded with most of her extended family, as well as Lorelei and her father—but maybe they'd been keeping something from her, waiting to break the bad news in person. . . .

Dr. Shane frowned, reading her face, which must have drained of all color. He even took a step toward her, perhaps fearing she might drop the infant girl, now resting her small head on Lizzie's shoulder. The child's body trembled with small, residual hiccoughs from the weeping. "Are you all right, Miss McKettrick?"

Lizzie consciously stiffened her backbone, a trick her grandfather had taught her. *Keep your back straight and your shoulders, too, Lizzie-girl, especially when you're scared.*

"I'm fine," she said, stalwart.

Dr. Shane gave a ghost of a grin. "Good, because we're in for a rough patch, and I'm going to need help."

As the shock subsided, the seriousness of the situation struck Lizzie like a second avalanche.

"I have to check on the engineer and the conductor," Dr. Shane told her, stepping up close now, in order to pass her in the narrow aisle.

Lizzie nodded. "We'll be rescued," she said, as

much for her own benefit as Dr. Shane's. Whitley wasn't listening; he'd taken a flask from his pocket and begun to imbibe in anxious gulps. The peddler and the soldier were talking in quiet tones, while Mrs. Halifax and her children huddled together in the quilt. The elderly couple spoke to each other in comforting whispers, Woodrow's cage spanning from one of their laps to the other like a bridge. "When we don't arrive in Indian Rock on schedule, folks will come looking for us."

Her father. Her uncles. Every able-bodied man and boy in Indian Rock, probably. All of them would saddle horses, hitch up sleighs, follow the tracks until they found the stalled train.

"Have you looked out the window, Lizzie?" Dr. Shane asked, sotto voce, as he eased past her and the shivering child. "We're miles from anywhere. We have at least eighteen feet of snow on one side, and a sheer cliff on the other. I'm betting heavily on first impressions, but you strike me as a sensible, level-headed girl, so I won't spare you the facts. We're in a lot of trouble—another snowslide could send us over the side. It would take an army to shovel us out, and one sick soldier does not an army make. We can't stay, and we can't leave. There's a full scale blizzard going on out there."

Lizzie swallowed, lifted her chin. Kept her backbone McKettrick straight. "I am not a girl," she said. "I'm nearly twenty, and I've earned a teaching certificate."

"Twenty?" the doctor teased dryly. "That old. And a schoolmarm in the bargain."

But Lizzie was again thinking of her family—her papa, her grandfather, her uncles. "They'll come," she said, with absolute confidence. "No matter what."

"I hope you're right," Dr. Shane said with a sigh, tugging at the sleeves of his worn coat in a preparatory sort of way. "Whoever 'they' are, they'd better be fast, and capable of tunneling through a mountain of snow to get to us. It will be pitch-dark before anybody even realizes this train is overdue, and since delays aren't uncommon, especially in this kind of weather, the search won't begin until morning—if then."

"Where's that laudanum?" Whitley whined. His cheeks were bright against his pale face. If Lizzie hadn't known better, she'd have thought he was consumptive.

Dr. Shane patted his medical bag. "Right here," he answered. "And it won't mix with that whiskey you're swilling. I'd pace myself, if I were you."

Whitley looked for all the world like a pretty child, pouting. What, Lizzie wondered abstractly, had she ever seen in him? Where was the dashing charm he'd exhibited in San Francisco, where he'd scrawled his name across her dance card at every party? Written her poetic love letters. Brought her flowers.

"Aren't you even going to examine him?" Lizzie asked, after some inward elbowing to get by her new opinion of Whitley's character. Oddly, given present circumstances, she reflected on her earlier and somewhat blithe conviction that he would settle in Indian Rock after they were married, so that she could teach and be near her family. He'd seemed casually agreeable to the idea of setting up house far from his own kin, but now that she thought about it, he'd never actually committed to that or anything else. "He might truly be hurt, you know."

"He's fine," Dr. Shane replied curtly. Then, medical kit in hand, he moved up the aisle, toward the locomotive.

"What kind of doctor is he, anyhow?" Whitley grumbled.

"One who expects to be very busy, I think," Lizzie said, not looking at him but at the door Dr. Shane had just shouldered his way through. She knew the car ahead was empty, and the locomotive was just beyond. She felt a little chill, because there had been no sign of the conductor since before the avalanche. Wouldn't he have hurried back to the only occupied passenger car to see if there were any injuries, if he wasn't hurt himself? And what about the engineer?

Suddenly she knew she had to follow Dr. Shane. Had to know, for her own sanity, just how dire the situation truly was. She moved to hand the baby girl to Whitley, but he shrank back as if she'd offered him a hissing rattlesnake in a peck basket.

Miffed, Lizzie took the child back to Mrs. Halifax, placed her gently on the woman's lap, tucked the quilt into place again. The peddler and the soldier were seated together now, playing a card game of some sort on the top of the sample case. The old gentleman left Woodrow in his wife's care and stood. "Is there anything I can do?" he asked, of everyone in general.

Lizzie didn't answer, but simply gave the old man a grateful smile and headed for the locomotive.

"Where are you going?" Whitley asked peevishly, as she passed.

She didn't bother to reply.

A cold wind knifed through her as she stepped out of the passenger car, and she could barely see for the snow, coming down furiously now, arching over the top of the train in an ominous canopy. The next car lay on its side, the heavy iron coupling once linking it to its counterpart snapped cleanly in two.

Lizzie considered retreating, but in the end a desperate need to know the full scope of their predicament overrode common prudence. She climbed carefully to the ground, using the ice-coated ladder affixed to one end of the car, and stooped to peer inside the overturned car.

It was an eerie sight, with the seats jutting out sideways. She uttered a soft prayer of gratitude that no one had been riding in that part of the train and crawled inside. Clutching the edge of the open luggage rack to her left, she straightened and crossed the car by stepping from the side of one seat to the next.

Finally, she reached the other door and steeled herself to go through the whole ordeal of climbing to the ground and reentering all over again.

The locomotive was upright, however, and the snow was packed so tightly between the two cars that it made a solid path. Lizzie moved across, longing for her fancy new coat, and stepped inside the engine room.

Steam huffed forlornly from the disabled boiler.

The conductor lay on the floor, the engineer beside him.

Dr. Shane, crouching between them, looked up at Lizzie with such a confounded expression on his face that, had things not been at such a grave pass, she would have laughed.

"You *said* you might need my help," she pointed out.

Dr. Shane snapped his medical bag closed, stood. He looked so glum that Lizzie knew without asking that the two men on the floor of the locomotive were either dead or mortally wounded.

Tears burned in her eyes as she imagined their families, preparing for Yuletide celebrations, unaware, as yet, that their eagerly awaited loved ones would never return.

"It was quick," Dr. Shane said, standing in front of her now, placing a hand on her shoulder. "Did you know them?"

Lizzie shook her head, struggling to compose herself. Her grandfather's deep voice echoed in her mind.

Keep your backbone straight—

"Were they—were they lying there, side by side like that?" It was a strange question, she knew that, even as she asked. Perhaps she was still in shock, after all. "When you found them, I mean?"

"I moved them," the doctor answered, "once I knew they were both gone."

Lizzie nodded. Just the act of standing up straight and squaring her shoulders made her feel a little better.

A slight, grim smile lifted the corner of Dr. Shane's finely-shaped mouth. "These rescuers you're expecting," he said. "If they're anything like you, we might have some hope of surviving after all."

Lizzie's heart ached. What she wouldn't have given to be at home on the Triple M at that moment, with her family all around her. There would be a big, fragrant tree in the parlor at the main ranch house, shimmering with tinsel. Dear, familiar voices, talking, laughing, singing. "Of course we'll survive," she heard herself say. Then she looked at the dead men again, and a lump lodged in her throat, so she had to swallow and then ratchet her chin up another notch before she could go on. "Most of us, anyway. My papa, my uncles, even my grandfather—they'll all come, as soon as they get word that the train didn't arrive."

"All of them McKettricks, I suppose."

Lizzie nodded again, shivering now. The boiler wasn't putting out any heat at all. Most likely, the smoke stack was full of snow. "They'll get through. You wait and see. Nothing stops a McKettrick, especially when there's trouble."

"I believe you, Miss McKettrick," he said.

"You must call me Lizzie," she replied, without thinking. He had, though only once, and she needed the normality of her given name. Just the sound of it gave her strength.

"Lizzie, then," Dr. Shane answered. "If you'll call me Morgan."

"Morgan," she repeated, feeling bewildered again.

He went back to the bodies, gently removed the conductor's coat, then laid it over Lizzie's shoulders. She shuddered inside it, at once grateful and repulsed.

"Let's get back to the others," Morgan said quietly. "There's nothing more we can do here."

Their progress was slow and arduous, but when they returned to the other car, someone had lighted lanterns, and the place had a reassuring glow. Most of the passengers seemed to have regained their composure. Even Woodrow had ceased his fussing; he peered alertly through the bars of his cage, his snow-white feathers smooth.

Whitley had emptied his flask and either passed out or gone to sleep, snoring loudly, clinging possessively to his blanket even in a state of unconsciousness.

"I'd better take a look at him," Morgan said ruefully, stopping by Whitley's seat and opening his kit, pulling a stethoscope from inside. "My preliminary diagnosis is pampering by an overprotective mother or a bevy of fussy aunts or spinster sisters, complicated by a fondness for strong spirits. I've been wrong before, though." But not very often, he might have added, if his tone was anything to go by.

Lizzie could not decide whether she liked this man or not. He certainly wasn't one to remain on the sidelines in a crisis, which was a point in his favor, but there was a suggestion of impatient arrogance about him, too. Clearly, he did not suffer fools lightly.

She approached the Halifax family and found them still burrowed down in the faded quilt. The peddler had lighted another cigar, and the soldier was on his feet, trying to see out into the night. Darkness, snow and the reflected light of the lanterns on the window glass made it pretty much impossible, but Lizzie understood his need to be doing something.

"Some Christmas this is going to be," he said, turning when Lizzie came to thank him for giving up his quilt to Mrs. Halifax and her little ones. "Nothing to eat, and it'll get colder and colder in here, you'll see."

"We'll need to keep our spirits up," Lizzie replied. "And expect the best." Lorelei said things generally turned out the way folks *expected* them to, Lizzie recalled, so it was important to maintain an optimistic state of mind.

"Reckon we ought to do both them things," the soldier said, his narrow, good-natured and plain face earnest as he regarded Lizzie. "But it wouldn't hurt to prepare for some rough times, either." He smiled, put out a hand. "John Brennan, private first class, United States Army," he said.

"Lizzie McKettrick," Lizzie replied, accepting the handshake. His palm and fingers felt dry and hot against her skin. Did he have a fever? "Do you live in Indian Rock, Mr. Brennan? I grew up on the Triple M, and I don't think I've ever seen you before."

"My wife's folks opened a mercantile there, six months ago. I was in an army hospital, back in Maryland, laid up with typhoid fever and the damage it done, for most of a year, so my Alice took our little boy and moved in with her mama and daddy to wait for my discharge." Sadness flickered in his eyes. "Reckon my boy's all het up about it bein' almost Christmas and all, and lookin' for me to walk through the front door any minute now."

Lizzie sat down in the aisle seat, and John Brennan lowered himself back into the one beside the window. Lorelei had written her about the new mercantile, pleased that they carried a selection of fine watercolors and good paper, among other luxuries, along with the usual coffee, dungarees, nails and tobacco products. "What's your boy's name?" she asked, "And how old is he?"

"He's called Tad, for his grandpappy," Mr. Brennan said proudly. "He turned four last Thursday. I was hoping to be home in time for the cake and candles, but my discharge papers didn't come through in time."

Lizzie smiled, thinking of her younger brothers. They'd be excited about Christmas, and probably watching the road for their big sister, even though they'd surely been told she'd arrive tomorrow. She consulted the watch pinned to her bodice; it was almost three o'clock. The train wasn't due in Indian Rock until six-fifteen.

She imagined her grandfather waiting impatiently in the small depot, right on time, hectoring the ticket clerk for news, ranting that in his day, everybody traveled by stagecoach, and by God, the coaches had been a hell of a lot more reliable than the railroad.

Shyly, John Brennan patted her hand. "I guess you've got home-folks waitin', too," he said.

Lizzie nodded. "Will you be working at the mercantile?" she asked, just to keep the conversation going. It was a lot less lonely that way. And a lot easier than thinking about the very real possibility of another avalanche, sending the whole train toppling over the cliff.

"Much as I'm able," Mr. Brennan replied. "Can't do any of the heavy work, loading and unloading freight wagons and such, but I've got me a head for figures. I can balance the books and keep track of the inventory."

"I'll be teaching at Indian Rock School when it reopens after New Year's," she said.

Mr. Brennan beamed. He was one of those

homely people who turn handsome when they smile. "In a couple of years, you'll have my Tad in first grade," he said. "Me and Alice, we place great store by book learnin' and such. Never got much of it myself, as you can probably tell by listenin' to me talk, but I learnt some arithmetic in the army. Tad, now, he'll go to school and make something of himself."

Lizzie remembered how Mr. Brennan had given his quilt to Mrs. Halifax, even though he was obviously susceptible to the cold. He'd wasted during his confinement, so that his uniform hung on his frame, and plans to help out at the mercantile or no, he might be a semi-invalid for a long time.

"If Tad is anything like his father," she said, "he'll do just fine."

Brennan flushed with modest pleasure. Sobered when he glanced toward the front of the train, where Whitley was awake again and complaining to Dr. Shane, who looked as though he'd like to throttle him. "Is that your brother?" he asked.

"Just someone I knew in San Francisco," Lizzie said, suddenly sad. The Whitley she'd thought she'd known so well had been replaced by a petulant impostor. She grieved for the man she'd imagined him to be—the young engineer, with great plans to build dams and bridges, the cavalier suitor with the fetching smile.

Morgan left Whitley and came back down the aisle. "I'm going out and have a look around," he said, addressing John Brennan instead of Lizzie. “If I don’t come back, don’t come searching for me.”

Lizzie stood up. “You can’t go out there alone,” she protested.

Morgan laid his hands on her shoulders and pressed her back into the hard, soot-blackened seat. “Mrs. Halifax might need you,” he said. “Or the children. Or the old folks—the husband has a bluish tinge around his lips, and I’m worried about his heart.” He paused, nodded toward Whitley. “God knows, that sniveling yahoo up there in the blanket won’t be any help.”

The peddler opened his sample case again, brought out a pint of whiskey, offered it to Morgan. “You may have need of this,” he said. “It’s mighty cold out there.”

Morgan took the bottle, put it in the inside pocket of his coat. “Thanks.”

“At least take one of the lanterns,” Lizzie said, anxious wings fluttering in her stomach, as though she’d swallowed a miniature version of Woodrow.

“I’ll do that,” Morgan answered.

“Here’s my hat,” Mr. Brennan said, holding out his army cap. “It ain’t much, but it’s better than going bare-headed.”

“I have a scarf,” Lizzie fretted. “It’s in my handbag—”

Morgan donned the cap. It looked incongruous indeed, with his worn-out suit, but it covered the tops of his ears. “I’ll be fine,” he insisted. He went back up the aisle, leaving his medical kit behind, and out through the door at the other end.

Lizzie watched for the glow of his lantern through the window, found it, lost track of it again. Her heart sank. Suppose he never came back? There were so many things that could happen out there in the frigid darkness, so full of the furious blizzard.

"I don't think your interest in the good doctor is entirely proper," a familiar voice said.

Lizzie looked up, mildly startled, and saw Whitley standing unsteadily in the aisle, glowering down at her. His cheeks were flushed, his eyes glazed.

"Be quiet," she said.

"We have an understanding, you and I," Whitley reminded her.

"I quite understand *you,* Whitley," Lizzie retorted, "but I don't think the reverse is true. Unless you mean to make yourself useful in some way, I'd rather you left me alone."

Whitley was just forming his reply when the whole car shuddered again, listed slightly cliffward, and caught. The peddler shouted a curse. Mr. Brennan launched into the Lord's Prayer. Mrs. Halifax gave a soblike gasp, and her children shrieked in chorus. Woodrow squawked and sidestepped along his perch, and the elderly couple clung to each other.

"We're all right," Lizzie said, surprising herself by how serenely she spoke. Inside, she was terrified. "Nobody move."

"Seems to me," observed the peddler, having

recovered a modicum of composure, "that we'd all better sit on the other side of the car."

"Good idea," Lizzie agreed.

Whitley took a seat very slowly, his face a ghastly white. Lizzie, the peddler, and John Brennan crossed the aisle carefully to settle in. So did the old folks and Woodrow.

Outside, the wind howled, and Lizzie thought she could feel the heartbeat of the looming mountain itself, ponderous and utterly impersonal.

Where was Morgan Shane?

Lost in the impenetrable snow? Buried under it?

Fallen into one of the treacherous crevasses for which the high country was well known?

Lizzie wanted to cry, but she knew it was an indulgence she couldn't afford. So she cleared her throat and began to sing, in a soft, tremulous voice, " 'God rest ye merry gentlemen, let nothing you dismay . . .' "

Slowly, tentatively, the others joined in.

Chapter Two

Morgan hadn't intended to wander far from the train—he'd meant to keep the lantern-light from the windows in view—but the storm was worse than he'd thought. Cursing himself for a fool, his own lantern having guttered and subsequently been tossed aside, he stood with the howling wind stinging his ears, bare hands shoved into the pockets of his inadequate coat. It was as though a veil had descended; he not only couldn't see the glow of the lamps, he couldn't see the train. All sense of direction deserted him—he might be a step from toppling over the rim of the cliff.

Be rational, he told himself. *Think.*

For the briefest moment the wind collapsed to a whisper, as though drawing another breath to blow again, and he heard a faint sound, a snatch of singing.

He pressed toward it, blinded by the pelting snow, blinked to clear his eyes and glimpsed the light shining through the train windows. Seconds later he collided hard against the side of the railroad car. Feeling his way along it, grateful even for the scorching cold of bare metal under his palms, he found the door.

Stiff-handed, he managed to open it and veritably *fall* inside. He dropped to his knees, steadied himself by grasping the arm rest of the nearest seat. His lungs burned, and the numbness began to recede from his hands and feet and face, leaving intense pain in its wake.

Frostbite? Suppose he lost his fingers? What good was a doctor and sometime surgeon without fingers?

He hauled himself to his feet and found himself face-to-face with a wide-eyed Lizzie McKettrick. He could have tumbled into the blue of those eyes; it seemed fathomless. She draped something around him—a blanket or a quilt or perhaps a cloak—and boldly burrowed into his coat pocket, brought out the pint the peddler had given him earlier.

Pulling the cork, she raised the bottle to his lips and commanded, "Drink this!"

He managed a couple of fiery swallows, waved away the bottle. His vision began to clear, and the thrumming in his ears abated a little. With a chuckle he ran a shaky forearm across his mouth. "If you have any kindness in your soul," he said laboriously, "you will not say 'I told you so.' "

"Very well," Lizzie replied briskly, "but I *did* tell you so, didn't I?"

He laughed. Not that anything was funny. He'd seen little on his foray into the blizzard, but he *had* confirmed a few of his worst suspicions. The car was off the tracks, and tipping with dangerous delicacy away from the mountainside. And *nobody,* McKettrick or not, was going to get through that weather.

If any of them survived, it would be a true miracle.

Once Morgan stopped shivering, Lizzie returned the quilt to Mrs. Halifax and went forward again to sit with him. Whitley glared at her as she passed his seat.

She'd gotten used to wearing the conductor's coat by then; even though it smelled of coal smoke and sweat, it was warm. She considered offering it to Morgan, but she knew he would refuse, so she didn't make the gesture.

"I heard you singing," Morgan said, somewhat distractedly, when she sat down beside him. "That's how I found my way back. I heard you singing."

Moved, Lizzie touched his hand tentatively, then covered it with her own. His skin felt like ice, and his clothes were damp. Once he dozed off, not that he was in any condition to stop her even then, she'd make her way back to the baggage car. Raid her trunks and crates, and Whitley's, too, for dry garments. And the freight car might contain food, matches, even blankets.

Lizzie's stomach rumbled. None of them had eaten since their brief stop in Flagstaff, hours before, and she'd picked at her leathery meat loaf and overcooked green beans. Left most of it behind. Now she would have devoured the sorry fare happily and ordered a cup of strong, steaming coffee.

Coffee.

Suddenly, she yearned for the stuff, generously laced with cream and sugar—and a good splash of brandy.

Morgan's fingers curled around hers, squeezed lightly. "Lizzie?"

"I was just thinking of hot coffee," she confessed, keeping her voice down, "and food. Do you suppose there might be food in the freight car?"

He grinned at her. "I watched you in the restaurant at the depot today," he said. "You barely touched your meat loaf special."

"You were watching me?" She found the idea at once disturbing and titillating.

"Hard not to," Morgan said. "You're a very good-looking woman, Lizzie. I did wonder, I confess, about your taste in traveling companions."

Lizzie felt color warm her cheeks, and for once, she welcomed it. Every other part of her was cold. "You seem to have formed a very immediate, and very poor, impression of Mr. Carson."

"I'm a good judge of character," he replied. "Mr. Carson doesn't seem to have one, as far as I've been able to discern."

"How could you possibly have reached such a conclusion merely by *looking* at him in a busy train depot?"

"He didn't pull back your chair for you when you sat down," Morgan went on, his tone just shy of smug. "And you paid the bill. It only took a glance to see those things—I saved the active looking for you."

"Mr. Carson," Lizzie said, mildly mortified, "is making this journey as my *guest.* That's why I paid for his meal. He is, I assure you, quite solvent."

"Planning to parade him past the McKettricks?" Morgan teased, after a capitulating grin. "I've only met one of them—Kade—a few weeks ago, in Tucson. He told me Indian Rock needed a doctor and offered me an office in the Arizona Hotel and plenty of patients if I'd come and set up a practice. Didn't strike me as the sort to be impressed by the likes of Mr. Carson."

All kinds of protests were brewing in Lizzie's

bosom, but the mention of her uncle's name stopped her as surely as the avalanche had stopped the train. Though she wasn't about to admit it, Morgan's guess was probably correct. Kade, like all the other McKettrick men, judged people by their actions rather than their words. Whitley could talk fit to charm a mockingbird out of its tree, but he plainly wasn't much for pushing up his sleeves and *doing* something about a situation. There was no denying that.

"I'm afraid you're right," Lizzie conceded, bereft.

Morgan squeezed her hand again.

The wind lashed at the train from the side that wasn't snowbound, rocked it ominously back and forth. Lizzie spoke again, needing to fill the silence.

"Did you practice medicine in Tucson?" she asked.

Morgan shook his head. "Chicago," he said, and then went quiet again.

"Are you going to make me do all the talking?" Lizzie demanded after an interval, feeling fretful.

That smile tilted the corner of his mouth again. "I'm no orator, Lizzie."

"Just tell me something about yourself. Anything. I'm pretty scared right now, and if you don't hold up your end of the conversation, I'll probably prattle until your ears fall off."

He chuckled. It was a richly masculine sound. "All right," he said. "My name, as you already know, is Morgan Shane. I'm twenty-eight years old. I was born and raised in Chicago—no brothers or sisters.

My father was a doctor, and that's why I became one. He studied in Berlin after graduating from Harvard, since, in his opinion, American medical schools were deplorable. So I went to Germany, too. I've never been married, though I came close once—her name was Rosalee. I practiced with my father until he died—probably would have stayed put, except for a falling-out with my mother. I decided to move west, and wound up in Tucson."

It was more information than Lizzie had dared hope for, and she felt her eyes widen. "What happened to Rosalee?" she asked, a little breathless, for she had a weakness for romance. Whenever she got the chance, she read love stories and sighed over the heroes. The woman must have died tragically, thereby breaking Morgan's heart and turning him into a wanderer, and perhaps the experience explained his terse way of speaking, too.

"She decided she'd rather be a doctor than a doctor's wife and went off to Berlin to study for a degree of her own. Or was it Vienna? I forget."

Lizzie's mouth fell open.

Morgan grinned again. "I'm teasing you, Lizzie. She eloped with a man who worked in the accounts receivable department at Sears and Roebuck."

She peered at him, skeptical.

He laughed. "Your turn," he said. "What do you plan to do with your life, Lizzie McKettrick?"

"I mean to teach in Indian Rock," Lizzie said, suddenly wishing she had a more interesting occupation to describe. A trapeze artist, perhaps, or a painter of stately portraits. A noble nurse, bravely battling all manner of dramatic diseases.

"Until you marry and start having babies."

Lizzie was rattled all over again. What *was* it about Morgan Shane that both nettled her and piqued her interest? "My uncle Jeb's wife is a teacher," she said defensively. "They have four children, and Chloe still holds classes in the country school house he built for her with his own hands." Jack and Ellen, living on the Triple M, would attend Chloe's classes, because the distance to town was too great to travel every day.

Morgan's eyes darkened a little as he assessed her, or seemed to. Maybe it was just a trick of the light. "How does Mr. Carson fit into all this?"

Lizzie sighed. Looked back over one shoulder to make sure Whitley wasn't eavesdropping. Instead he'd gone back to sleep. "I thought I wanted to marry him," she answered, in a whisper.

"Why?"

"Well, because it seemed like a good idea, I guess. I'm almost twenty. I'd like to start a family of my own."

"While continuing to teach?"

"Of course," Lizzie said. "I know what you think—that I'll have to choose one or the other. But I don't have to choose."

"Because you're a McKettrick?"

Again, Lizzie's cheeks warmed. "Yes," she said,

quite tartly. "Because I'm a McKettrick." She huffed out a frustrated breath. "And because I'm strong and smart and I can do more than one thing well. No one would think of asking *you* when you'd give up being a doctor and start keeping house and mending stockings, if you decided to get married, would they?"

"That's different, Lizzie."

"No, it isn't."

He settled back against the seat, closed his eyes. "I think I'm going to like Indian Rock," he said. And then he went to sleep, leaving Lizzie even more confounded than before.

"I have to use the chamber pot," a small voice whispered, startling Lizzie out of a restless doze. "And I can't find one."

Opening her eyes, Lizzie turned her head and saw the little Halifax girl standing in the aisle beside her. The last of the lanterns had gone out, and the car was frigid, but the blizzard had stopped, and a strangely beautiful bluish light seemed to rise from the glittering snow. Everyone else seemed to be asleep.

Recalling the spittoon she'd seen at the back of the car, Lizzie stood and took the child's chilly hand. "This way," she whispered.

The business completed, the little girl righted her calico skirts and said solemnly, "Thanks."

"You're welcome," Lizzie replied softly. She could have used a chamber pot herself, right about then, but she wasn't about to use the spittoon. She escorted the child back to her seat, tucked part of Mr. Brennan's quilt around her.

"We have to get home," the little girl said, her eyes big in the gloom. "St. Nicholas won't be able to find us out here in the wilderness, and Papa promised me I'd get a doll this year because I've been so good. When Mama had to tie a string to my tooth to pull it, I didn't even cry." She hooked a finger into one corner of her small mouth to show Lizzie the gap. "Schee?" she asked.

Lizzie's heart swelled into her throat. She looked with proper awe upon the vacant spot between two other teeth, shook her head. Wanting to gather the child into her arms and hold her tightly, she restrained herself. Children were skittish creatures. "I think *I* would have cried, if I had one of *my* teeth pulled," she said seriously. She'd actually seen that particular extraction process several times, back on the ranch—it was a brutal business but tried and true. And usually quick.

"My papa works on the Triple M now," the little girl went on proudly. "He just got hired, and he's foreman, too. That means we get our own house to live in. It has a fireplace and a real floor, and Mama says we can hang up Papa's socks, if he has any clean ones, he's been batching so long, and St. Nicholas will put an orange in the toe. One for me, and one for Jack, and one for Nellie Anne."

Lizzie nodded, still choked up, but smiling gamely. "Your brother is Jack," she said, marking the names in her memory by repeating them aloud, "and the baby is Nellie Anne. What, then, is *your* name?"

The small shoulders straightened. "Ellen Margaret Halifax."

Lizzie put out a hand in belated introduction. "Since I'll be your teacher, you should probably call me Miss McKettrick," she said.

"Ellen," Mrs. Halifax called, in a sleepy whisper, "you'll freeze standing there in the aisle. Come get back under the quilt."

Ellen obeyed readily, and soon gave herself up to dreams. From the slight smile resting on her mouth, Lizzie suspected the child's imagination had carried her home to the foreman's house on the Triple M, where she was hanging up a much-darned stocking in anticipation of a rare treat—an orange.

Having once awakened, Lizzie found she could not go back to sleep.

The baggage and freight cars beckoned.

Morgan, the one person who might have stopped her from venturing out of the passenger car, slumbered on.

Resolutely, Lizzie buttoned up the conductor's coat, extracted a scarf from her hand luggage and tied it tightly under her chin, in order to protect her ears from a cold she knew would be merciless.

Once ready, she crept to the back of the car, struggled with the door, winced when it made a slight creaking sound. A quick glance back over one shoulder reassured her. None of the other passengers stirred.

The cold, as she had expected, bit into her flesh like millions of tiny teeth, but the snow had stopped coming down, and she could see clearly in the light of the moon. The car was still linked to the one behind it, and both remained upright.

Shivering on the tiny metal platform between the two cars, Lizzie risked a glance toward the cliff and was alarmed to see how close the one she'd just left had come to pitching over the edge.

Her heart pounded; for a moment she considered rushing back to awaken the others, herd them into the baggage car, which was, at least, still sitting on the tracks.

But would the second car be any safer?

It was too cold to stand there deliberating. She shoved open the next door. They would all be better able to deal with the crisis if she found food, blankets, *anything* to keep body and soul together until help arrived.

And help *would* arrive. Her father and uncles were probably on their way even then. The question was, would they get there before there was another snowslide, before everyone perished from the unrelenting cold?

Lizzie found her own three steamer trunks, each of them nearly large enough for her to stand up inside, stacked one on top of the other. A pang struck her. Papa had teased her mercilessly about traveling with so much luggage. *You'd never make it on a cattle drive,* he'd said.

God, how she missed Holt McKettrick in that moment. His strength, his common sense, his innate ability to deal ably with whatever adversity dared present itself.

Think, Lizzie, she told herself. *Fretting is useless.*

Chewing on her lower lip, she pondered. Of course the coat and her other woolen garments were in the red trunk, and it was on the bottom. If she dislodged the other two—which would be a Herculean feat in its own right, involving much climbing and a lot of pushing—would the inevitable jolts send the passenger car, so precariously tilted, plummeting to the bottom of the ravine?

She decided to proceed to the freight car and think about the trunks on the way back. It was very possible, after all, that orders of blankets and coats and stockings and—please, God, *food*—might be found there, originally destined for the mercantile in Indian Rock, thus alleviating the need to rummage through her trunks.

Getting into the freight car proved impossible—the door was frozen shut, and no amount of kicking, pounding and latch wrenching availed. She finally lowered herself to the ground, by means of another small ladder, and the snow came up under her skirts to soak through her woolen bloomers and sting her thighs. She was perilously close to the edge, too—one slip and she would slide helplessly down the steep bank.

At least the hard work of moving at all warmed her

a bit. Clinging to the side of the car with both hands, she made her precarious way along it. Her feet gave way once, and only her numb grip on the iron edging at the base of the car kept her from tumbling to her death.

After what seemed like hours, she reached the rear of the freight car. Somewhere in the thinning darkness, a wolf howled, the sound echoing inside Lizzie, ancient and forlorn.

Buck up, she ordered herself. *Keep going.*

Behind the freight car was the caboose, painted a cheery red. And, glory be, a *chimney* jutted from its roof. Where there was a chimney, there was a stove, and where there was a stove—

Blessed warmth.

Forgoing the freight car for the time being, Lizzie decided to explore the caboose instead.

She had to wade through more snow, and nearly lost her footing again, but when she got to the door, it opened easily. She slipped inside, breathless, teeth chattering. Somewhere along the way, she'd lost her scarf, so her ears throbbed with cold, fit to fall right off her head.

There *was* a stove, a squat, pot-bellied one, hardly larger than the kettle Lorelei used for rendering lard at home. And on top of that stove, miraculously still in place after the jarring impact of the avalanche, stood a coffee pot. Peering inside a small cupboard near the stove, she saw a few precious provisions—a tin of coffee, a bag of sugar, a wedge of yellow cheese.

Lizzie gave a ranch-girl whoop, then slapped a hand over her mouth. Raised in the high country from the time she was twelve, she knew that when the snow was so deep, any sudden sound could bring most of the mountainside thundering down on top of them. She listened, too scared to breathe, for an ominous rumble overhead, but none came.

She assessed the long, benchlike seats lining the sides of the car. Room for everyone to lie down and sleep.

Yes, the caboose would do nicely.

She forced herself to go outside again—even the sight of that stove, cold as it was, had warmed her a little. The freight car proved as impenetrable from the rear door as from the first one Lizzie had tried, but she was much heartened, just the same. Morgan, Whitley and the peddler would be able to get inside.

She was making her way back along the side of the train, every step carefully considered, both hands grasping the side, when it happened.

Her feet slipped, her stomach gave a dull lurch, and she felt herself falling.

She slid a few feet, managed to catch hold of a tree root, the tree itself long gone. Fear sent the air whooshing from her lungs, as if she'd been struck in the solar plexus, and she knew her grip would not last long. She had almost no feeling in her hands, and her feet dangled in midair. She did not dare turn her head and look down.

"Help me!" she called out, in a voice that sounded laughably cheerful, given the circumstances.

Morgan's head appeared above her, a genie sprung from a lamp. "Hold on," he told her grimly, "and *do not* move."

She watched, blinking salty moisture from her eyes, as he unbuckled his belt, pulled it free of his trousers and fashioned a loop at one end. He lay down on his belly and tossed the looped end of the belt within reach.

"Listen to me, Lizzie," he said very quietly. "Take a few breaths before you reach for the belt. You can't afford to miss."

Lizzie didn't even nod, so tenuous was her hold on the root. She took the advised breaths, even closed her eyes for a moment, imagined herself standing on firm ground. Safe with Morgan.

If she could just get to Morgan. . . .

"Ready?" he asked.

"Yes," she said. Still clinging to the root, which was already giving way, with one hand, she grasped the leather loop with the other. Morgan's strength seemed to surge along the length of it.

"I've got you, Lizzie," Morgan said. "Take hold with the other hand."

After another deep breath, she let go of the root.

Morgan pulled her up slowly, and very carefully. When she crested the bank, he hauled her into his arms and held her hard, both of them kneeling only inches from the lip of the cliff.

"Easy, now," he murmured, his breath warming her right ear. "No sudden moves."

Lizzie nodded slightly, her face buried in his shoulder, clinging to the fabric of his coat with both hands.

Morgan rose carefully to his feet, bringing Lizzie with him.

"The caboose," she said, trembling all over. "There's a stove in the caboose—and a c-coffeepot."

He took her there. Seated her none too gently on one of the long seats. "What the *hell* were you thinking?" he demanded, moving to the stove, stuffing in kindling and old newspaper from the half-filled wood box, striking a match to start a blaze.

"I was looking for food . . . blankets—"

Morgan gave her a scathing look. Took the coffeepot off the stove and went out the rear door of the caboose. When he came back, Lizzie saw that he'd filled the pot with snow. He set it on the stove with an eloquent clunk. "You could have been killed!" he rasped, pale with fury.

"How did you know to . . . to come looking for me?"

"John Brennan woke me up. Said he'd seen you leave the car. At first, he thought he was dreaming, because nobody would do anything that stupid."

"*You* left the car," Lizzie reminded him. "What's the difference?"

"The *difference,* Lizzie McKettrick, is that you are a woman and I am a man. And don't you *dare* get up on a soapbox. If I hadn't come along when I did, you'd be at the bottom of that ravine by now. And it was the grace of—whoever—that we didn't *both* go over!"

He found a tin of coffee among the provisions, spooned some into the pot, right on top of the snow.

Lizzie realized that he'd put himself in no little danger to pull her to safety. "Thank you," she said, with a peculiar mixture of graciousness and chagrin.

"I'm not ready to say 'you're welcome,'" he snapped. "Leaving that car, especially alone, was a damnably foolish thing to do."

"If you expect an apology, Dr. Shane, you will be sorely disappointed. Someone had to do something."

The fire crackled merrily in the stove, and a little heat began to radiate into the frosty caboose. Morgan reached up to adjust the damper, still seething.

"Don't talk," he advised, sounding surly.

Lizzie straightened her spine. "Of course I'm going to talk," she told him pertly. "I have things to say. We need to bring everyone from the passenger car. It's safer here—and warmer."

"*We* aren't going to do anything. *You* are going to stay put, and *I* will go back for the others." He leveled a long look at her. "So help me God, Lizzie, if you set foot outside this caboose—"

She smiled, getting progressively warmer, catching the first delicious scent of brewing coffee. She'd probably imagined that part, she decided.

"Why, Dr. Shane," she mocked sweetly, batting her

eyelashes, "I wouldn't *think* of disobeying a strong, capable man like you."

Suddenly he laughed. Some of the tension between them, until that moment tight as a rope with an obstreperous calf running full out at the other end, slackened.

It gave Lizzie an odd feeling, not unlike dangling over the side of a cliff with only a root to hold on to and the jaws of a ravine yawning below.

She blushed. Then her practical side reemerged. "I tried the door on the freight car," she said. "But I couldn't get in. If we're lucky, there might be food inside."

"Oh, we're lucky, all right," Morgan responded, his amusement fading as reality overtook him again. The sun was coming up, and Lizzie knew as well as he did that even its thin, wintry warmth might thaw some of the snow looming over their heads, set it to sliding again. "We're lucky we're alive." He studied her for a long moment. Then he snapped, "Wait here."

Frankly not brave enough to risk another plunge over the cliff-side, McKettrick or not, Lizzie waited. Waited when he left. Waited for the coffee to brew.

He brought the baby first.

Lizzie held little Nellie Anne and bit her lip, waiting.

Next came Jack, riding wide-eyed on Morgan's shoulders, his little hands clasped tightly under the doctor's chin.

After that, Mrs. Halifax. Her arm still in its sling, she fairly collapsed, once safely inside the caboose. Lizzie immediately got up to fill a coffee mug and hand it to the other woman. Mrs. Halifax trembled visibly as she drank, her two older children clutching at her skirts.

Whitley appeared, having made his own way, scowling. Still clutching his blanket, he looked even more like an overgrown child than before. When Mrs. Halifax gave him a turn with the cup, he added a generous dollop from his flask and glared at Lizzie while he drank. She'd seen him empty the vessel earlier; perhaps he had a spare bottle in his valise.

She did her best to ignore him, but it was hard, since he seemed determined to make his stormy presence felt.

The peddler arrived next, escorting the old woman, his jowls red with the cold. He'd brought his sample case, too, and he immediately produced a cup of his own, from the case, and poured a cup of coffee at the stove. "Hell of a Christmas," he boomed, to the company in general, understandably cheered by the warmth from the fire and probably dizzy with relief at having made the treacherous journey between cars unscathed. He gave the cup to the elderly lady, who took it with fluttery hands and quiet gratitude.

Finally, John Brennan came, on his feet but supported by Morgan. The old man accompanied them, carrying Woodrow's covered cage.

The peddler, after flashing a glance Whitley's way,

conjured more cups from his sample case, shiny new mugs coated in blue enamel, and gave them to the newer arrivals.

"I'm starving," Whitley said petulantly. "Is there any food?"

"Starving!" Woodrow commented from his cage.

The grin Morgan turned on Whitley was anything but cordial. "I thought maybe we could count on you, hero that you are, to hike out with a rifle and bag some wild game," he said.

Whitley reddened, looked for a moment as though he might fling aside the coffee mug he was hogging and go for Morgan's throat. Apparently, he thought better of it, though, for he remained seated, taking up more than his share of room on the benchlike seat opposite Lizzie. Muttered something crude into his coffee.

Lizzie stood, approached Morgan. "I was thinking if we could find a way to—well, *unhook* this car from the next—"

"Stop thinking," Morgan interrupted. "It only gets you in trouble."

Lizzie felt as though she'd been slapped. "But—"

Morgan softened, but only slightly. Regarded her over the rim of his steaming coffee. "Lizzie," he said, more gently, "it's a question of weight. As shaky as our situation is, if we uncoupled the cars, we'd be *more* vulnerable, separated from the rest of the train, not less."

He was right, which only made his words harder

for Lizzie to swallow. She averted her eyes, only to have her gaze land accidentally on Whitley. He was smirking at her.

She lifted her chin, turned away from both Whitley and Morgan, and set about helping Mrs. Halifax make a bed for the children, using John Brennan's quilt. That done, she turned to the elderly couple.

Their names were Zebulon and Marietta Thaddings, Lizzie soon learned; they lived in Phoenix, but Mrs. Thaddings's sister worked in Indian Rock, and they'd intended to surprise her with a holiday visit. Having no one to look after Woodrow in their absence, they'd brought him along.

"He's a good bird," Mrs. Thaddings said sweetly. "No trouble at all."

Lizzie smiled at that. "Perhaps I know your sister," she said.

Mrs. Thaddings beamed. "Perhaps you do," she agreed. "Her name is Clarinda Adams, and she runs a dressmaking business."

Lizzie felt a pitching sensation in the pit of her stomach. There was no dressmaker in Indian Rock, but there *was* a very exclusive "gentleman's club," and Miss Clarinda Adams ran it. Cowboys could not afford what was on offer in Miss Adams's notorious establishment, but prosperous ranchers, railroad executives and others of that ilk flocked to the place from miles around to drink imported brandy, play high-stakes poker and dandle saucy women on their knees.

Oh, Miss Adams was going to be surprised, all right, when the Thaddingses appeared on her doorstep, with a talking bird in tow. But the Thaddingses would be even more so.

Lizzie felt a flash of mingled pity and amusement. She patted Mrs. Thaddings's hand, still chilled from the perilous journey from one railroad car to another, and offered to refill her coffee cup.

Once they'd finished off the coffee and started a second pot to brewing, Morgan and the peddler set out to break into and raid the freight car.

As soon as they were gone, Whitley approached Lizzie, planted himself directly in front of her.

"If I die," he told her, "it will be *your fault.* If you hadn't insisted on bringing me into this wilderness to meet your family—"

Despite a dizzying sting—for there was truth in his words, as well as venom—Lizzie kept her backbone straight, her shoulders back and her chin high. "After staying alive," she said, with what dignity she could summon, "my biggest problem will be *explaining* you to my family."

With a snort of disgust, he turned on one heel and strode to the other side of the car.

And little Ellen tugged at the sleeve of the oversize conductor's coat Lizzie had been wearing since the day before. "Do you think St. Nicholas will know where we are?" she asked, her eyes huge with worry. "Jack's had a mean hankerin' for that orange ever since Mama told us we could hang up stockings this year."

"I'm absolutely certain St. Nicholas will know *precisely* where we are," Lizzie told Ellen, laying a hand on her shoulder. "But we'll be in Indian Rock by Christmas Eve, you'll see."

Would they? Ellen looked convinced. Lizzie, on the other hand, was beginning to have her doubts.

Chapter Three

The caboose, although not much safer than the passenger car, was at least warm. When Morgan and the peddler returned from their foray, they brought four gray woolen blankets, as many tins of canned food, all large, and a box of crackers.

"There was a ham," the peddler blustered, red from the cold and loud with relief to be back within the range of the stove, "but the doc here said it was probably somebody's Christmas dinner, special-ordered, so we oughtn't to help ourselves to it."

Everyone nodded in agreement, including Ellen and Jack, her younger brother. Only Whitley looked unhappy about the decision.

There were no plates and no utensils. Morgan opened the tins with his pocket knife, and they all ate of the contents—peaches, tomatoes, pears and a pale-skinned chicken—forced to use their hands. When the meal was over, Morgan found an old bucket next to the stove and carried in more snow, to be melted on the stove, so they could wash up.

While it was a relief to Lizzie to assuage her

hunger, she was still restless. It was December twenty-third. Her father and uncles must be well on their way to finding the stalled train. She yearned for their arrival, but she was afraid for them, too. The trip from Indian Rock would be a treacherous one, cold and slow and very hard going, most of the way. For the first time it occurred to her that a rescue attempt might not avert calamity but invite it instead. Her loved ones would be putting their lives at risk, venturing out under these conditions.

But venture they would. They were McKettricks, and thus constitutionally incapable of sitting on their hands when somebody—especially one of their own—needed help.

She closed her eyes for a moment, willed herself not to fall apart.

She thought of Christmas preparations going on at the Triple M. There were four different houses on the ranch, and the kitchens would be redolent with stove heat and the smells of good things baking in the ovens.

By now, having expected to meet her at the station in Indian Rock the night before, her grandfather would definitely have raised the alarm. . . .

She started a little when Morgan sat down on the train seat beside her, offered her a cup of coffee. She'd drifted homeward, in her musings, and coming back to a stranded caboose and a lot of strangers was a painful wrench.

She saw that the others were all occupied: John

Brennan sleeping with his chin on his chest, Ellen and Jack playing cards with the peddler, Whitley reading a book—he always carried one in the inside pocket of his coat—Mrs. Halifax modestly nursing baby Nellie Anne beneath the draped quilt. Mrs. Thaddings had freed Woodrow from his cage, and he sat obediently on her right shoulder, a well-behaved and very observant bird, occasionally nibbling a sunflower seed from his mistress's palm.

"Brennan," Morgan told Lizzie wearily, keeping his voice low, "is running a fever."

Lizzie was immediately alarmed. "Is it serious?"

"A fever is *always* serious, Lizzie. He probably took a chill between here and the other car, if not before. From the rattle in his chest, I'd say he's developing pneumonia."

"Dear God," Lizzie whispered, thinking of the little boy, Tad, waiting to welcome his father at their new home in Indian Rock.

"Giving up hope, Lizzie McKettrick?" Morgan asked, very quietly.

She sucked in a breath, shook her head. *"No,"* she said firmly.

Morgan smiled, squeezed her hand. "Good."

Lizzie had seen pneumonia before. While she'd never contracted the dreaded malady herself, she'd known it to snatch away a victim within days or even hours. Concepcion, her stepgrandmother, and Lorelei had often attended the sick around Indian Rock and in the bunkhouses on the Triple M, and

Lizzie had kept many a vigil so the older women could rest. "I'll help," she said now, though she wondered where she was going to get the strength. She was young, and she was healthy, but her nerves felt raw, exposed—strained to the snapping point.

"I know," Morgan said, his voice a little gruff. "You would have made a fine nurse, Lizzie."

"I don't have the patience," she replied seriously, wringing her hands. They'd thawed by then, along with all her other extremities, but they ached, deep in the bone. "To be a nurse, I mean."

Morgan arched one dark eyebrow. "Teaching doesn't require patience?" he asked, smiling.

Lizzie found a small laugh hiding somewhere inside her, and allowed it to escape. It came out as a ragged chuckle. "I see your point," she admitted. She turned her head, saw Ellen and Jack enjoying their game with the peddler, and smiled. "I love children," she said softly. "I love the way their faces light up when they've been struggling with some concept and it suddenly comes clear to them. I love the way they laugh from deep down in their middles, the way they smell when they've been playing in summer grass, or rolling in snow—"

"Do you have brothers and sisters, Lizzie?"

"Brothers," she said. "All younger. John Henry—he's deaf and Papa and Lorelei adopted him after his folks were killed in Texas, in an Indian raid. Lorelei, that's my stepmother, sent away for some special books from back east, and taught him to talk with his hands. Then she taught the rest of us, too. Gabe and Doss learned it so fast."

"I'll bet you did, too," Morgan said. By the look in his eyes, Lizzie knew his remark wasn't intended as flattery. Unless she missed her guess, Dr. Morgan Shane had never flattered anyone in his life. "John Henry is a lucky little boy, to be a part of a family like yours."

"We've always thought it was the other way around," Lizzie said. "John Henry is so funny, and so smart. He can ride any horse on the ranch, draw them, too, so you think they'll just step right off the paper and prance around the room, and when he grows up, he means to be a telegraph operator."

"I'm looking forward to meeting him, along with the rest of the McKettricks," Morgan told her. His gaze had strayed to Whitley, narrowed, then swung back to Lizzie's face.

Something deep inside her leapt and pirouetted. Morgan wanted to meet her family. But of course it *wasn't* because he had any personal interest in her. Her uncle Kade had encouraged him to come to Indian Rock to practice medicine, and the McKettricks were leaders in the community. Naturally, as a newcomer to town, Morgan would seek to make their acquaintance. Her heart soaring only moments before, she now felt oddly deflated.

Morgan stood. "I'd better go outside again," he said. "See what I can round up in the way of fuel. What firewood we have isn't going to last long, but there's a fair supply of coal in the locomotive."

Lizzie hated the thought of Morgan braving the dangerous cold again, but she knew he had to do it, and she was equally certain that he wouldn't let her go in his stead. Still, she caught at his hand when he would have walked away, looked up into his face. "How can I help, Morgan?"

His free hand moved, lingered near her cheek, as though he might caress her. But the moment passed, and he did not touch her. "Maybe you could rig up some kind of bed for John, on one of these bench seats," he said quietly. "He used up most of his strength just getting here. He's going to need to lie down soon."

Lizzie nodded, grateful to have something practical to do.

Morgan left.

Lizzie sat a moment or so longer, then stood, straightening her spine vertebra by vertebra as she did. Fat flakes of snow drifted past the windows of the train, and the sky was darkening, even though it was only midday.

Papa, she thought. *Hurry. Please, hurry.*

Lizzie made up John Brennan's makeshift bed on one of the benches, as near to the stove as she could while still leaving room for her or Morgan to attend to him. He gave her a grateful look when she awakened him from an uncomfortable sleep and helped him across the car to his new resting place. Using two of the four blankets from the freight car as pillows, she tucked him in between the remaining pair. Laid a hand to his forehead.

His skin was hot as a skillet forgotten over a campfire.

"I could do with some water," he told Lizzie. "My canteen is in my haversack, but it's been empty for a while."

Lizzie nodded. "Dr. Shane brought in some snow a while ago. I'll see if it's melted yet."

"Thank you," Mr. Brennan said. And then he gave a wracking cough that almost bent him double.

"Is he contagious?" Whitley wanted to know. He stood at her elbow, his book dangling in one hand.

"I only wish he were," Lizzie answered coolly. "Then you might catch some of his good manners and his generosity."

"Don't you think we should stop bickering?" Whitley retorted, surprising her. "After all, we're all in danger here, the way that sawbones tells it."

"Are you just realizing that, Whitley?" Lizzie asked. "And Dr. Shane is not a 'sawbones.' He's a *physician,* trained in Berlin."

"Well, huzzah for him," Whitley said bitterly. Apparently, his suggestion that they make peace had extended only as far as Lizzie herself. *He* was going to go right on being nasty. "I swear he's turned your head, Lizzie. You're smitten with him. And you don't know a damn thing about the man, except what he's told you."

"I know," Lizzie said moderately, "that when this

train was struck by an avalanche, he didn't think of *himself* first."

Whitley's color flared. "Are you implying that I'm a coward?"

The peddler, Ellen and Jack looked up from their game.

John Brennan went right on coughing.

Woodrow, back in his cage, spouted, "Coward!"

"No," Lizzie replied thoughtfully. "I've watched you play polo, and you can be quite brave. Maybe 'reckless' would be a better term. But you are selfish, Whitley, and that is a trait I cannot abide."

He gripped her shoulders. Shook her slightly. "Now you can't 'abide' me?" he growled. "Why? Because you're a high-and-mighty McKettrick?"

A click sounded from somewhere in the car, distinctive and ominous.

Lizzie glanced past Whitley and saw that the peddler had pointed a small handgun in their direction.

"Unhand the lady, if you please," the man said mildly.

Ellen and Jack stared, their eyes enormous.

"Don't shoot," Lizzie said calmly.

Whitley's hands fell to his sides, but the look on his face was cocky. "So you're still fond of me?" he asked Lizzie.

"No," Lizzie replied, watching his obnoxious grin fade as the word sank in. "I'm not the least bit fond of you, Whitley. But a shot could start another avalanche."

Whitley reddened.

The peddler lowered the pistol, allowing it to rest on top of his sample case, under his hand.

"I'm catching the first train out of this godforsaken country!" Whitley said, shaking a finger under Lizzie's nose. "I should have known you'd turn out to be—to be *wild.*"

Lizzie drew in her breath. " 'Wild'? If you're trying to insult me, Whitley, you're going to have to do better than *that.*" She jabbed at his chest with the tip of one index finger. "And kindly *do not* shake your finger at me!"

The peddler chuckled.

"Wild!" Woodrow called shrilly. "Wild!"

The door at the rear of the caboose opened, and Morgan came in, stomping snow off his boots. He carried several broken tree branches in his arms, laid them down near the stove to dry, so they could be burned later. His gaze came directly to Lizzie and Whitley.

"I'm leaving!" Whitley said, forcing the words between his teeth.

"That might be difficult," Lizzie pointed out dryly, "since we're *stranded.*"

"I won't stay here and be insulted!"

"You'd rather go out there and die of exposure?"

"You think I'm a coward? I'm *selfish?* Well, I'll show you, Lizzie McKettrick. I'll follow the tracks until I come to a town and get help—since your high-falutin *family* hasn't shown up!"

"You can't do that," Morgan said, the voice of irritated moderation. "You wouldn't make it a mile, whether you followed the tracks or not. Anyhow, in case you haven't been listening, the tracks are *buried* under snow higher than the top of your head."

"Maybe you're afraid, *Dr.* Shane, but I'm not!" Whitley looked around, first to the peddler, then to poor John Brennan. "I think we should *all* go. It would be better than sitting around in this caboose, waiting to fall over the side of a mountain!"

Ellen raised a small hand, as though asking a question in class. "Are we going to fall over the mountain?" she asked. Jack nestled close against his sister's side, pale, and thrust a thumb into his mouth.

"You're frightening the children!" Lizzie said angrily.

Morgan raised both hands in a bid for peace. "We're *not* going to fall off the mountain," he told the little girl and Jack, his tone gentle. But when he turned to Whitley, his eyes blazed with temper. "If you want to be a damn fool, *Mr.* Carson, that's your business. But don't expect the rest of us to go along with you."

Little Jack began to cry, tears slipping silently down his face, his thumb still jammed deep into his mouth.

"Stop that," Ellen told him, trying without success to dislodge the thumb. "You're not a baby."

Whitley grabbed up his blanket, stormed across the

car and flung it at Ellen and Jack. Then he banged out of the caboose, leaving the door ajar behind him.

Lizzie took a step in that direction.

Morgan closed the door. "He won't get far," he told her quietly.

"Come here to me, Jack," Mrs. Halifax said. She'd finished feeding and burping the baby, laid her gently on the seat beside her; Nellie Anne was asleep, reminding Lizzie of a cherub slumbering on a fluffy cloud.

Jack scrambled to his mother, crawled onto her lap.

Lizzie felt a pinch in her heart. She'd held her youngest brother, Doss, in just that way, when he was smaller and frightened by a thunderstorm or a bad dream.

"I have some goods in the freight car," the peddler said, tucking away the pistol, securing his case under the seat and rising. He buttoned his coat and went out.

Lizzie helped Ellen gather the scattered cards from their game. Mrs. Halifax rocked Jack in her lap, murmuring softly to him.

Morgan checked the fire, added wood.

"He'll be back," he told Lizzie, when their gazes collided.

He was referring to Whitley, of course, off on his fool's errand.

Lizzie nodded glumly and swallowed.

When the peddler returned, he was lugging a large wooden crate marked Private in large, stenciled letters. He set it down near the stove, with an air of mystery, and Ellen was immediately attracted. Even Jack slid down off his mother's lap to approach, no longer sucking his thumb.

"What's in there?" the little boy asked.

The peddler smiled. Patted the crate with one plump hand. Took a handkerchief from inside his coat and dabbed at his forehead. Remarkably, in that weather, he'd managed to work up a sweat. "Well, my boy," he said importantly, straightening, "I'm glad you asked that question. Can you read?"

Jack blinked. "No, sir," he said.

"I can," Ellen piped up, pointing to a label on the crate. "It says, 'Property of Mr. Nicholas Christian.' "

"That," the peddler said, "would be me. Nicholas Christian, at your service." He doffed his somewhat seedy bowler hat, pressed it to his chest and bowed. He turned to Jack. "You ask what's in this box? Well, I'll tell you. *Christmas.* That's what's in here."

"How can a whole day fit inside a box?" Ellen demanded, sounding at once skeptical and very hopeful.

"Why, child," said Nicholas Christian, "Christmas isn't merely a *day.* It comes in all sorts of forms."

Morgan, having poured a cup of coffee, watched the proceedings with interest. Mrs. Halifax looked troubled, but curious, too.

"Are you going to open it?" Jack wanted to know. He was practically breathless with excitement. Even

John Brennan had stirred upon his sickbed to sit up and peer toward the crate.

"Of course I am," Mr. Christian said. "It would be unthinkably rude not to, after arousing your interest in such a way, wouldn't you say?"

Ellen and Jack nodded uncertainly.

"I'll need that poker," the peddler went on, addressing Morgan now, since he was closest to the stove. "The lid of this box is nailed down, you know."

Morgan brought the poker.

Woodrow leaned forward on his perch.

The peddler wedged one end of it under the top of the crate and prized it up with a squeak of nails giving way. A layer of fresh wood shavings covered the contents, hiding them from view.

Lizzie, preoccupied with Whitley's announcement that he was going to follow the tracks to the nearest town, looked on distractedly.

Mr. Christian knelt next to the crate, rubbed his hands together, like a magician preparing to conjure a live rabbit or a white-winged dove from a hat, and reached inside.

He brought out a shining wooden box with gleaming brass hinges. Set it reverently on the floor. When he raised the lid, a tune began to play. "O little town of Bethlehem . . ."

Lizzie's throat tightened. The works of the music box were visible, through a layer of glass, and Jack and Ellen stared in fascination.

"Land," Ellen said. "I ain't—" she blushed, looked up at Lizzie "—I *haven't* never seen nothin' like this."

Lizzie offered no comment on the child's grammar.

"It belonged to my late wife, God rest her soul," Mr. Christian said and, for a moment, there were ghosts in his eyes. Leaving the music box to play, he plunged his hands into the crate again. Brought out a delicate china plate, chipped from long and reverent use, trimmed in gold and probably hand-painted. "There are eight of these," he said. "Spoons and forks and butter knives, too. We shall dine in splendor."

"What's 'dine'?" Jack asked.

Ellen elbowed him. "It means eating," she said.

"We ain't got nothin' to eat," Jack pointed out. By then, the crackers and cheese Lizzie had found in the cupboard were long gone, as were the canned foods pirated from the freight car.

"Oh, but we do," replied Mr. Christian. "We most certainly do."

The children's eyes all but popped.

"We have goose liver pâté." He produced several small cans to prove it.

Woodrow squawked and spread his wings.

Jack wrinkled his nose. "Goose liver?"

Ellen nudged him again, harder this time. "Whatever patty is," she told him, "it's vittles for sure."

"Pah-tay," the peddler corrected, though not

unkindly. "It is fine fare indeed." More cans came out of the box. A small ham. Crackers. Tea in a wooden container. And wonderful, rainbow-colored sugar in a pretty jar.

Lizzie's eyes stung a little, just watching as the feast was unveiled. Clearly, like the things stashed in her travel trunk, these treasures had been intended for someone in Indian Rock, awaiting Mr. Christian's arrival. A daughter? A son? Grandchildren?

"Of course, having recently enjoyed a fine repast," Mr. Christian said, addressing Ellen and Jack directly, but raising his voice just enough to carry to all corners of the caboose, "we'd do well to save all this for a while, wouldn't we?"

"I don't like liver," Jack announced, this time managing to dodge the inevitable elbow from Ellen. "But I wouldn't mind havin' some of that pretty sugar."

Morgan chuckled, but Lizzie saw him glance anxiously in the direction of the windows.

"Later," Mr. Christian promised. "Let us savor the anticipation for a while."

Both children's brows furrowed in puzzlement. The peddler might have been speaking in a foreign language, using words like *repast* and *savor* and *anticipation.* Raised hardscrabble, though, they clearly understood the concept of *later.* Delay was a way of life with them, young as they were.

Lizzie moved closer to Morgan, spoke quietly, while the music box continued to play. "Whitley," she said, "is an exasperating fool. But we can't let him wander out there. He'll die."

Morgan sighed. "I was just thinking I'd better go and bring him back before he gets lost."

"I'm going, too. It's my fault he's here at all."

"You're needed here," Morgan replied reasonably, with a slight nod of his head toward John Brennan. "I can't be in two places at once, Lizzie."

"I wouldn't know what to do if Mr. Brennan had a medical crisis," Lizzie said. "But I *do* know how to follow railroad tracks."

Morgan rested his hands on Lizzie's shoulders, just lightly, but a confounding sensation rushed through her, almost an ache, stirring things up inside her. "You're too brave for your own good," he said. "Stay here. Get as much water down Brennan as you can. Make sure he stays warm, even if the fever makes him want to throw off his blankets."

"But what if he—?"

"What if he dies, Lizzie? I won't lie to you. He might. But then, so might all the rest of us, if we don't keep our heads."

"You're exhausted," Lizzie protested.

"If there's one thing a doctor learns, it's that exhaustion is a luxury. I can't afford to collapse, Lizzie, and believe me, I won't."

Wanting to cling to him, wanting to make him stay, even if she had to make a histrionic scene to do it, Lizzie forced herself to step back. To let go, not just physically, but emotionally, too. "All right," she said.

"But if you're not back within an hour or two, I *will* come looking for you."

Morgan sighed again, but a tiny smile played at the corner of his mouth, and something at once soft and molten moved in his eyes. "I'll keep that in mind," he said. And then, after making only minimal preparations against the cold, he left the caboose.

Lizzie went immediately to the windows, watched him pass alongside the train. *Keep him safe,* she prayed silently. *Please, keep him safe. And Whitley, too.*

John Brennan began to cough. Lizzie fetched one of the cups, dashed outside to fill it with snow, set it on the stove. The chill bit deep into her flesh, gnawed at her bones.

Ellen and Jack whirled like figure skaters to the continuing serenade of the music box, Mr. Christian having demonstrated that it could play many different tunes, by virtue of small brass disks inserted into a tiny slot. Woodrow seemed to dance, inside his cage. Mr. and Mrs. Thaddings took in the scene, smiling fondly.

"I'm burnin' up," Mr. Brennan told Lizzie, when she came to adjust his blankets. "I need to get outside. Roll myself in that snow—"

Lizzie shook her head. She had no medical training, nothing to offer but the soothing presence of a woman. "That's your fever talking, Mr. Brennan," she said. "Dr. Shane said to keep you warm."

"It's like I'm on fire," he said.

How, Lizzie wondered, did people stand being nurses and doctors? It was a sore trial to the spirit to look helplessly upon human suffering, able to do so little to relieve it. "There, now," she told him, near to weeping. "Rest. I'll fetch a cool cloth for your forehead."

"That would be a pure mercy," he rasped.

Lizzie took her favorite silk scarf from her valise, steeled herself to go outside yet again.

Mr. Thaddings stopped her. Took the scarf from her hands and made the journey himself, shivering when he returned.

The snow-dampened scarf proved a comfort to Mr. Brennan, though the heat of his flesh quickly defeated the purpose. Lizzie, on her knees beside the seat where he lay, turned her head and saw that Zebulon Thaddings had brought in a bucketful of snow. Gratefully, she repeated the process.

"It would be a favor if you'd call me by my given name," Mr. Brennan told her. His coughing had turned violent, and he seemed almost delirious, alternately shaking with chills and trying to throw off his covers. "I wouldn't feel so far from home thataways."

Lizzie blinked back another spate of hot tears. "You'll get home, John," she said, fairly choking out the words. "I promise you will."

A small hand came to rest on her shoulder. She looked around, saw Ellen standing beside her. "I could do that," the child said gently, referring to the repeated wetting, wringing and applying of the cloth to John's forehead. "So you could rest a spell. Have some of that tea Mr. Christmas made."

Lizzie's first instinct was to refuse—tending the sick was no task for a small child. On the other hand, the offer was a gift and oughtn't to be spurned. "Mr. Christmas?" she asked, bemused, distracted by worry. "Don't you mean Mr. Christian?"

Ellen smiled, took the cloth. Edged Lizzie aside. "Here, now, Mr. Brennan," the little girl said, sounding like a miniature adult. "You just listen, and I'll talk. Me and my ma and my brother Jack and my little sister, Nellie Anne, we're on our way to the Triple M Ranch—"

Lizzie got to her feet, turned to find Mr. Christian holding out a mug full of spice-fragrant tea, hot and strong and probably laced with the very expensive colored sugar.

Mr. Christmas. Maybe Ellen had gotten the peddler's name right after all.

Chapter Four

The cold was brutal, the snow blinding. Morgan slogged through it, following the rails as best he could. It was in large part a guessing game, and he had to be careful to stay away from the bank on the left. That presented a challenge, since he couldn't be entirely certain where it was.

Carson, the damn fool, had left footprints, but they

were filling in fast, and the man was clearly no relation to the famous scout with the same last name. Tracking him was more likely to lead Morgan to the bottom of the ravine than the nearest town.

Cursing under his breath—the wind buffeted it away every time he raised his head—Morgan kept going, ever mindful of the passing of time. If he took too long finding Carson and bringing him back, he knew Lizzie would make good on her threat to mount a one-woman search. John Brennan was too sick to stop her, let alone make the trek in her stead, and the peddler, well, he was a curious fellow, now guarding that sample case of his as if it contained the Holy Grail, now serving up goose liver pâté and other delicacies on fancy china plates. He might keep Lizzie in the caboose, where she belonged, or send her out into the blizzard with his blessings. Morgan, by necessity an astute observer of the human animal, wasn't sure the man was completely sane.

Lizzie. In spite of his own situation, he smiled. What a hardheaded little firebrand she was—pretty. Smart as hell. Calm in a crisis that would have had many females—and males, too, to be fair—wringing their handkerchiefs and bewailing a cruel fate. He hadn't been joking when he'd said she'd make a good nurse.

Now, in the strange privacy of a high-country blizzard, he could admit something else, too—if only to himself. Lizzie McKettrick would make an even better doctor's wife than she would a nurse.

He felt something grind inside him, both painful and pleasant.

It was sheer idiocy to think of her in such intimate terms. They barely knew each other, after all, and she was set on teaching school, married or single. On top of that, she'd been fond enough of Whitley Carson to bring him home to her family during a sacred season. Her irritation with Carson would most likely fade, once they were all safe again. She'd forget the man's shortcomings soon enough, when the two of them were sipping punch beside a big Christmas tree in some grand McKettrick parlor.

The realization sobered Morgan. He felt something for Lizzie, though it was far too soon to know just what, but opening his time-hardened heart to her would be foolhardy. Rash. Until this trip, Morgan Shane had never done anything rash in his life. A week ago, even a few *days* ago, he wouldn't have considered taking the kind of stupid chance he was in the midst of right now, bumbling into the maw of a storm that might well swallow him whole.

Yes, he was a doctor, and a dedicated one. He was a pragmatist's pragmatist, in a field where the most competent were bone skeptical. He believed that, upon reaching the age of reason, everyone was responsible for their own actions, and the resultant consequences. Therefore, if Whitley Carson was stupid enough to set off looking for help in the middle of a snowstorm, he had that right. From Morgan's perspective, his own duty, as a man and as a physician, lay with John Brennan, Mrs. Halifax and her children, the peddler, the Thaddingses, and Lizzie.

Hell, he even felt responsible for the bird.

So why was he out there in the snowstorm, when he knew better, knew the hopelessness of the task he'd undertaken?

The answer made him flinch inside.

Because of Lizzie. He was doing this for Lizzie. Whatever her present mood, she loved Carson. Bringing the man home to the bosom of her fabled clan was proof of that.

Flesh stinging, Morgan kept walking. His feet were numb, and so were his hands. His ears burned as though someone had laid hot pokers to them, and every breath felt like an inhalation of flame. He fumbled for the flask Nicholas Christian had given him earlier, managed to get the lid off, and took a swig, blessing the bracing warmth that surged through him with the first swallow.

He found Carson sprawled in the snow, just around a bend.

Was he dead?

Morgan's heartbeat quickened, and so did his half-frozen brain. He crouched beside the prone body, searched for and found a pulse.

Carson opened his eyes. "My leg," he scratched out. "I think I've broken my leg . . . slipped on the tracks . . . almost went over the side—"

Morgan confirmed the diagnosis with a few practiced motions of his hands, even though his wind-stung eyes had already offered the proof. He opened the flask again, with less difficulty this time, and held it to Carson's lips. "I'll get you back to the train," he said, leaning in close to be heard over the howl of the wind, "but it's going to hurt."

Carson swallowed, nodded. "I know," he rasped. He groaned when Morgan hoisted him to his one good foot, cried out when he tried to take a step.

Morgan sighed inwardly, crouched a little, and slung Carson over his right shoulder like a sack of grain. He remembered little of the walk back to the train—it was a matter of staying upright and putting one foot in front of the other. At some point, Carson must have passed out from the pain—he was limp, a dead weight, and several times Morgan had to fight to keep from going down.

When the train came in sight, Morgan offered a silent prayer of thanks, though it had been a long time since he'd been on speaking terms with God. The peddler, Mr. Christian, met him at the base of the steps leading up to the caboose. Stronger than Morgan would have guessed, the older man helped him get the patient inside.

Lizzie had concocted something on the stove—a soup or broth of some sort, from the savory aroma, but when she saw her unconscious beau, alarm flared in her eyes and she turned from the coffee can serving as an improvised kettle. "Is he . . . he's not—"

Morgan shook his head to put her mind at ease, but didn't answer verbally until he and the peddler had laid their burden down on the bench seat opposite the place where John Brennan rested.

"His leg is broken," Morgan said grimly, rubbing his hands together in a mostly vain attempt to restore some circulation. He had a small supply of morphine in his bag, along with tincture of laudanum—he'd sent his other supplies ahead to Indian Rock after agreeing to set up a practice there. He could ease Carson's pain, but he dared not give him too much medicine, mainly because the damned fool had been tossing back copious amounts of whiskey since the avalanche. "I have to set the fracture," he added. "For that, I'll need some straight branches and strips of cloth to bind them to the leg."

Lizzie drew nearer, peering between Morgan and the peddler to stare, white-faced, at Carson. "Is he in pain?" she asked, her voice small.

No one answered.

"I'll see what I can find for splints," the peddler said.

Morgan replied with a grateful nod. He'd nearly frozen, hunting down and retrieving Carson. If he went out again too soon, he'd be of no use to anybody. "Stay near the train if you can," he told Christian. "And take care not to slip over the side."

The peddler promised to look out for himself and left. Mrs. Halifax and the children were sleeping, all of them wrapped up together in the quilt. Mr. and

Mrs. Thaddings were snoozing, too, the sides of their heads touching, though Woodrow was wide-awake and very interested in the proceedings.

"When your friend regains consciousness, he'll be in considerable pain," Morgan said, in belated answer to Lizzie's question. Her concern was only natural—anyone with a shred of compassion in their soul would be sympathetic to Carson's plight. Still, the intensity of her reaction, unspoken as it was, reconfirmed his previous insight—Lizzie might *think* she no longer loved Whitley Carson, but she was probably fooling herself.

She did something unexpected then—took Morgan's hands into her own, removed the gloves he'd borrowed from Christian earlier, chafed his bare, cold skin between warm palms. The act was simple, patently ordinary and yet sensual in a way that Morgan was quite unprepared to deal with. Heat surged through him, awakening nerves, rousing sensations in widely varying parts of his anatomy.

"I've made soup," Lizzie told him, indicating the coffee can on the stove, its contents bubbling cheerfully away. Morgan recalled the tinned ham from the peddler's crate and the dried beans from the freight car. "You'd better have some," she added. "It will warm you up."

She'd warmed him up plenty, but there was no proper way to explain that. Numb before, Morgan ached all over now, like someone thawing out after a bad case of frostbite. "Best get Mr. Carson ready for the splints," he said. "The more I can do before he wakes up, the better."

She nodded her understanding, but dipped a clean mug into the brew anyway, and brought the soup to Morgan. He took a sip, set the mug aside, shrugged out of his coat. Using scissors from his bag, he cut Carson's snow-soaked pant leg from hem to knee and ripped the fabric open to the man's midthigh. Lizzie neither flinched nor looked away.

Morgan had the brief and disturbing thought that Lizzie might not be unfamiliar with the sight of Carson's bare flesh. He shoved the idea aside—Lizzie McKettrick's private life was patently none of his business. He certainly had no claim on her.

"I've got a petticoat," she said.

The announcement startled Morgan. Meanwhile, Carson had begun to stir, writhing a little, tossing his head from side to side as, with consciousness, the pain returned. Morgan paused to glance at Lizzie.

She went pink. "To bind the splints," she explained.

Morgan nodded, trying not to smile at her embarrassment.

Lizzie stepped back, out of his sight. There followed a poignantly feminine rustle of fabric, and then she returned to present him with a garment of delicate ivory silk, frothing with lace. For one self-indulgent moment, Morgan held the petticoat in a tight fist, savoring the feel of it, the faint scent of lavender caught in its folds, then proceeded to rip the costly fabric into wide strips. In the interim, Lizzie fetched his bag without being asked.

Carson opened his eyes, gazed imploringly up at her. "I meant . . ." he whispered awkwardly, the words scratching like sandpaper on splintery wood. "I meant to find help, Lizzie. . . . I'm so sorry . . . the way I acted before . . ."

"Shh," she said. She sat down on the bench, carefully placed Carson's head on her lap, stroked his hair. Morgan felt another flash of envy, a deep gouge of emotion, raw and bitter.

Christian returned with the requested tree branches, trimmed them handily with an ivory-handled pocket knife. The scent of pine sap lent the caboose an ironically festive air.

"This is going to hurt," Morgan warned Carson bluntly, gripping the man's ankle in both hands.

Carson bit his lower lip and nodded, preparing himself.

"Can't you give him something for the pain?" Lizzie interceded, looking up into Morgan's face with anxious eyes.

"Afterward," Morgan said. He didn't begrudge Carson a dose of morphine, but it was potent stuff, and the patient was in shock. If he happened to be sensitive to the drug, as many people were, the results could be disastrous. Better to administer a swallow of laudanum later. "It'll be over quickly."

"Do it," Carson said, and went up a little in

Morgan's estimation. Perhaps he had some character after all.

Morgan closed his eyes; he had a sixth sense about bones and internal organs, something he'd never mentioned to a living soul, including his father, because there was no scientific explanation for it. He saw the break in his mind, as clearly as if he'd laid Carson's hide and muscle open with a scalpel. When he felt ready, he gave the leg a swift, practiced wrench.

Carson yelled.

But the fractured femur was back in alignment.

Quickly, deftly, and with all the gentleness he could manage—again, this was more for Lizzie's sake than Carson's—Morgan set the splints in place and bound them firmly with the long strips of petticoat.

Taking a bottle of laudanum from his kit, Morgan pulled the cork and held it to Carson's mouth. "One sip," he said.

Sweating and pale, Carson raised himself up a little from Lizzie's lap and gulped down a mouthful of the bitter compound. The drug began taking effect almost immediately—Carson sighed, settled back, closed his eyes. Lizzie murmured sweet, senseless words to him, still smoothing his hair.

Morgan had set many broken limbs in his time, but this experience left him oddly enervated. He couldn't look at Lizzie as he put the vial of laudanum back in his kit, took out his stethoscope. There was something intensely private about the way she ministered to Carson, as tenderly as a mother with a child.

Or a wife with a husband.

Morgan turned away quickly, the stethoscope dangling from his neck, and crossed the railroad car to check Mr. Thaddings's heart, which thudded away at a blessedly normal rate, then moved on to examine John Brennan again.

"How are you feeling?" he asked the soldier gruffly. The question was a formality; the feverish glint in Brennan's eyes and the intermittent shivers that seemed to rattle his protruding skeleton provided answer enough.

Brennan's voice was a hoarse croak. "I heard that feller yell—"

"Broken leg," Morgan said. "Don't fret over it."

A racking cough tore itself from the man's chest. When he'd recovered, following a series of wheezing gasps, Brennan reached out to clasp at Morgan's hand, pulled. Morgan leaned down.

Brennan rasped out a ragged whisper. "I got to stay alive long enough to see my boy again," he pleaded. "It's almost Christmas. I can't have Tad recalling, all his life, that his pa passed. . . ." The words fell away as another spate of coughing ensued.

Morgan crouched alongside the bench seat, since there were no chairs in the caboose. He was not accustomed to smiling under the best of circumstances, so the gesture came a lot harder that day. Brennan had one foot dangling over an open grave, and unless some angel grabbed him by the coattails and held on tight, he was sure to topple in.

"You'll be all right," he said. "Don't think about dying, John. Think about *living.* Think about fishing with your son—about better times—" Much to his surprise, Morgan choked up. Had to stop talking and work hard at starting again. He couldn't remember the last time he'd lost control of his emotions—maybe he never had. *If you're going to be any damned use at all,* he heard his father say, *you've got to keep your head, no matter what's going on around you.*

"My wife," John said, laboring to utter every word, "makes a fine rum cake, every Christmas—starts it way down in the fall—"

"You suppose she baked one this year?" Morgan asked quietly, when he could speak.

John smiled. Managed a nod. As hard as talking was for him, he seemed comforted by the exchange. Probably he was clutching one end of the conversation for dear life, much as Lizzie had held on to Morgan's looped belt earlier, when she'd slipped in the snow. "She doubled the receipt," he ground out. "Just 'cause I was going to be home for Christmas."

Morgan noted the old-fashioned word *receipt*—his family's cook, Minerva, had used that term, too, in lieu of the more modern *recipe*—and then registered Brennan's use of the past tense. "You'll be there, John," he said.

Exhausted, John settled back, seemed to relax a

little. His gaze drifted, caught on someone, and Morgan realized Lizzie was standing just behind him. She held a mug of steaming ham and bean soup and one of the peddler's fancy spoons.

Morgan straightened, glanced back at Carson, who seemed to be sleeping now, though fitfully. Sweat beaded the man's forehead and upper lip, and Morgan knew the pain was biting deep, despite the laudanum.

"I thought Mr. Brennan might require some sustenance," she said, her eyes big and troubled. She'd paled, and her luscious hair drooped as if it would throw off its pins at any moment and tumble down around her shoulders, falling to her waist.

Morgan nodded, stepped back out of the way.

Lizzie moved past him, her arm brushing his as she went by, and knelt alongside Brennan. "It would be better with onions," she said gamely, holding a spoonful of the brew to the patient's lips. "And salt, too." When he opened his mouth, she fed him.

"Them beans is sure bony," Brennan said. "I guess they ain't had time to cook through."

Lizzie gave a rueful little chuckle of agreement.

And Morgan watched, struck by some stray and nameless emotion.

It was a simple sight, a woman spooning soup into an invalid's mouth, but it stirred Morgan just the same. He wondered if Lizzie would fall apart when this was all over, or if she'd carry on. He was betting on the latter.

Of course, they'd have to be rescued first, and the worse the weather got, the more unlikely that seemed.

The thin soup soothed Brennan's cough. He accepted as much as he could and finally sank into a shallow rest.

Creeping shadows of twilight filled the car; another day was ending.

The peddler had engaged the children in a new game of cards. Carson, like Brennan, slept. Mrs. Halifax and the baby lay on the bench seat, bundled in the quilt, the woman staring trancelike into an uncertain future, the infant gnawing on one grubby little fist.

Madonna and Child, Morgan thought glumly.

He made his way to the far end of the car, sat down on the bench and tipped his head back against the window. Tons of snow pressed cold against it, seeped through flesh and bone to chill his marrow; he might have been sitting in the lap of the mountain itself. He closed his eyes; did not open them when he felt Lizzie take a seat beside him.

"Rest," he told her. "You must be worn-out."

"I can't," she said. He heard the slightest tremor in her voice. "I thought—I thought they'd be here by now."

Morgan opened his eyes, met Lizzie's gaze.

"Do you suppose something's happened to them? My papa and the others?"

He wanted to comfort her, even though he shared

her concern for the delayed rescue party. If they'd set out at all, they probably hadn't made much progress. He took her hand, squeezed it, at a loss for something to say.

She smiled sadly, staring into some bright distance he couldn't see. "Tomorrow is Christmas Eve," she said, very quietly. "My brothers, Gabriel and Doss, always want to sleep in the barn on Christmas Eve, because our grandfather says the animals talk at midnight. Every year they carry blankets out there and make beds in the straw, determined to hear the milk cows and the horses chatting with each other. Every year they fall asleep hours before the clock strikes twelve, and Papa carries them back into the house, one by one, and Lorelei tucks them in. And every year, I think this will be the time they manage to stay awake, the year they stop believing."

Morgan longed to put an arm around Lizzie's shoulders and draw her close, but he didn't. Such gestures were Whitley Carson's prerogative, not his. "What about you?" he asked. "Did you sleep in the barn on Christmas Eve when you were little? Hoping to hear the animals talk?"

She started slightly, coming out of her reverie, turning to meet his eyes. Shook her head. "I was twelve when I came to live on the Triple M," she said.

She offered nothing more, and Morgan didn't pry, even though he wanted to know everything about her, things she didn't even know about herself.

"You've been a help, Lizzie," he told her. "With John Brennan and with Carson, too."

"I keep thinking about the conductor and the engineer—their families. . . ."

"Don't," Morgan advised.

She studied him. "I heard what you told John Brennan—that he ought to think about fishing with his son, instead of . . . instead of dying—"

Morgan nodded, realized he was still holding Lizzie's hand, improper as that was. Drew some satisfaction from the fact that she hadn't pulled away.

"Do you believe it really makes a difference?" she went on, when she'd gathered her composure. "Thinking about good things, I mean?"

"Regardless of how things turn out," he replied, "thinking about good things feels better than worrying, wouldn't you say? So in that respect, yes, I'd say it makes a difference."

She pondered that, then looked so directly, and so deeply, into his eyes that he felt as though she'd found a peephole into the wall he'd constructed around his truest self. "What are *you* thinking about, then?" she wanted to know. "You must be worried, like all the rest of us."

He couldn't tell Lizzie the truth—that despite his best efforts, every few minutes he imagined how it would be, treating patients in Indian Rock, with her at his side. "I can't afford to worry," he said. "It isn't productive."

She wasn't going to let him off the hook; he could

see that. Her blue eyes darkened with determination. “What was Christmas like for you, when you were a boy?”

Morgan found the question strangely unsettling. His father had been a doctor, his mother an heiress and a force of nature, especially socially. During the holiday season, they’d gone to, or given, parties every night. “Minerva—she was our cook—always roasted a hen.”

Lizzie blinked. Waited. And finally, when certain that nothing more was forthcoming, prodded, “That’s all? Your cook roasted a chicken? No tree? No presents? No carols?”

“My mother wouldn’t have considered dragging an evergreen into the house,” Morgan admitted. “In her opinion, the practice was crass and vulgar—and besides, she didn’t want pitch and birds’ nests all over the rugs. Every Christmas morning, when I came to the breakfast table, I found a gift waiting on the seat of my chair. It was always a book, wrapped in brown paper and tied with string. As for carols—there was a church at the end of our street, and sometimes I opened a window so I could hear the singing.”

“That sounds lonely,” Lizzie observed.

His childhood Christmases had indeed been lonely, Morgan reflected. Which made December 25 just like the other 364 days of the year. For a moment he was a boy again, he and Minerva feasting solemnly in the kitchen of the mansion, just the two of them. His dedicated father was out making a house call, his mother sleeping off the effects of a merry evening passed among the strangers she preferred to him.

"If you hadn't mentioned a cook," Lizzie went on, when he didn't speak, "I would have thought you'd grown up in a hovel."

He smiled at that. His mother had regarded him as an inconvenience, albeit an easily overlooked one. She'd often rued the day she'd married a poor country doctor instead of a financier, like her late and sainted sire, and made no secret of her regret. Morgan's father had endured by staying away from home as much as possible, often taking his young son along on his rounds when he, Morgan, wasn't locked away in the third-floor nursery with some tutor. Those excursions had been happy ones for Morgan, and he'd seen enough suffering, visiting Elias Shane's patients, most of them in tenements and charity hospitals, to know there were worse fates than growing up with a spoiled, disinterested and very wealthy mother.

He'd had his father, to an extent.

He'd had Minerva. She'd been born a slave, Minerva had. To her, Lincoln's Emancipation Proclamation was as sacred as Scripture. She'd actually met the man she'd called "Father Abraham," after the fall of Richmond. She'd clutched at the sleeve of his coat, and he'd smiled at her. *Such sorrow in them gray, gray eyes,* she'd told Morgan, who never tired of the much-told tale. *Such sadness as you'd never credit one man could hold.*

Morgan withdrew from the memory. He'd have given a lot to hear that story just one more time.

Lizzie bit her lip. Took fresh notice of his threadbare clothes, then caught herself and flushed a fetching pink. "You're *not* poor," she concluded, then colored up even more.

He laughed, and damn, it felt good. "Oh, but I am, Lizzie McKettrick," he said. "Poor as a church mouse. Mother didn't mind so much when I went to Germany to study. She figured it would pass, and I'd come to my senses. When I came home and took up medicine in earnest, she disinherited me."

Lizzie's marvelous eyes widened again. "She did? But surely your father—"

"She showed him the door, too. She was furious with him for encouraging me to become a doctor instead of overseeing the family fortune. Minerva opened a boarding house, and Dad and I moved in as her first tenants. We found a storefront, hung out a shingle and practiced together until Dad died of a heart attack."

Sorrow moved in Lizzie's face at the mention of his father's death. She swallowed. "What became of your mother?" she asked, sounding meek now, in the face of such drama.

"She sold the mansion and moved to Europe, to escape the shame."

"What shame?"

God bless her, Morgan thought, she was actually confused. "In Mother's circles," he said, "the practice of medicine—especially when most of the patients can't pay—is not a noble pursuit. She could have forgiven herself for marrying a doctor—youthful passions, lapses of judgment, all that—but when I decided to become a physician instead of taking over my grandfather's several banks, it was too much for her to bear."

"I'm sorry, Morgan," Lizzie said.

"It isn't as if we were close," Morgan said, touched by the sadness in Lizzie McKettrick's eyes as he had never been by Eliza Stanton Shane's indifference. "Mother and I, I mean."

"But, still—"

"I had my father. And Minerva."

Lizzie nodded, but she didn't look convinced. "My mother died when I was young. And even though I'm close to Lorelei—that's my stepmother—I still miss her a lot."

He couldn't help asking the question. It was out of his mouth before he could stop it. "Is money important to you, Lizzie?" He'd told her he was poor, and suddenly he needed to know if that mattered.

She glanced in Carson's direction, then looked straight into Morgan's eyes. "No," she said, with such alacrity that he believed her instantly. There was no guile in Lizzie McKettrick—only courage and sweetness, intelligence and, unless he missed his guess, a fiery temper.

He wanted to ask if Whitley Carson would be able to support her in the manner to which she was clearly accustomed, considering the fineness of her clothes and her recently acquired education, but he'd recovered his manners by then.

"Miss McKettrick?"

Both Lizzie and Morgan turned to see Ellen standing nearby, looking shy.

"Yes, Ellen?" Lizzie responded, smiling.

"I can't find a spittoon," Ellen said.

Lizzie chuckled at that. "We'll go outside," she replied.

"A spittoon?" Morgan echoed, puzzled.

"Never mind," Lizzie told him.

"I believe I'll go, too," Mrs. Halifax put in, rising awkwardly from her bed on the bench because of her injured arm, wrapping her shawl more closely around her shoulders.

Lizzie bundled Ellen up in the peddler's coat, readily volunteered, and the trio of females braved the snow and the freezing wind. The baby girl stayed behind, kicking her feet, waving small fists in the air, and cooing with sudden happiness. She'd spotted the cockatiel with the ridiculous name. What was it?

Oh, yes. Woodrow.

"I reckon we ought to be sparing with the kerosene," the peddler told Morgan, nodding toward the single lantern bravely pushing back the darkness. "Far as I could see when we checked the freight car, there isn't a whole lot left."

Morgan nodded, finding the prospect of the coming night a grim one. When the limited supply of firewood was gone, they could use coal from the bin in the locomotive, but even that wouldn't last more than a day or two.

The little boy, Jack, like Brennan and Carson, had fallen asleep.

The peddler spoke in a low voice, after making sure he wouldn't be overheard. "You think they'll find us in time?"

Morgan shoved a hand through his hair. "I don't know," he said honestly.

"You know anything about Miss Lizzie's people?"

Morgan frowned. "Not much. I met her uncle, Kade, down in Tucson."

"I've heard of Angus McKettrick," Christian confided, his gaze drifting briefly to Whitley Carson's prone and senseless form before swinging back to Morgan. "That's Miss Lizzie's grandpa. Tough as an army mule on spare rations, that old man. The McKettricks have money. They have land and cattle, too. But there's one thing that's more important to them than all that, from what I've been told, and that's kinfolks. They'll come, just like Miss Lizzie says they will. They'll come because she's here—you can be sure of that. I'm just hoping we'll all be alive and kicking when they show up."

Morgan had no answer for that. There were no guarantees, and plenty of dangers—starvation, for one. Exposure, for another. And the strong likelihood of a second, much more devastating, avalanche.

"You figure one of us ought to try hiking out of here?"

Morgan looked at Carson. "*He* didn't fare so well," he said.

"He's a greenhorn and we both know it," the peddler replied.

"How far do you think we are from Indian Rock?"

"We're closer to Stone Creek than Indian Rock," Christian said. "Tracks turn toward it about five miles back. It's another ten miles into Stone Creek from there. Probably twenty or more to Indian Rock from where we sit."

Morgan nodded. "If they're not here by morning," he said, "I'll try to get to Stone Creek."

"You're needed here, Doc," the peddler said. "I'm not as young as I used to be, but I've still got some grit and a good pair of legs. Know this country pretty well, too—and you don't."

Lizzie, Mrs. Halifax and Ellen returned, shivering. Lizzie struggled to shut the caboose door against a rising wind.

Morgan and the peddler let the subject drop.

They extinguished the lamp soon after that, ate ham and "bony" bean soup in the dark.

Everyone found a place to sleep.

And when Morgan opened his eyes the next morning, at first light, he knew the snow had stopped. He sat up, looked around, found Lizzie first. She was still sleeping, sitting upright on the bench seat, bundled in a blanket. John Brennan hadn't wakened, and neither had Mrs. Halifax and her children. Whitley Carson, a book in his hands, stared across the car at him with an unreadable expression in his eyes.

"The peddler's gone," he told Morgan. "He left before dawn."

Chapter Five

Lizzie dreamed she was home, waking up in her own room, hearing the dear, familiar sounds of a ranch house morning: stove lids clattering downstairs in the kitchen; the murmur of familiar voices, planning the day. She smelled strong coffee brewing, and wood smoke, and the beeswax Lorelei used to polish the furniture.

Christmas Eve was special in the McKettrick household, but the chores still had to be done. The cattle and horses needed hay and water, the cows required milking, the wood waited to be chopped and carried in, and there were always eggs to be gathered from the henhouse. Behind the tightly closed doors of Papa's study, she knew, a giant evergreen tree stood in secret, shimmering with tinsel strands and happy secrets. The luscious scent of pine rose through the very floorboards to perfume the second floor.

Throughout the day, the uncles and aunts and cousins would come, by sleigh or, if the roads happened to be clear, by team and wagon and on horseback. There would be exchanges of food, small gifts, laughter and stories. In the evening, after attending church services in town, they would all gather at the main house, where Lizzie's grandfather Angus would read aloud, his voice deep and resonant, from the Gospel of Luke.

And there were in the same fields, shepherds, guarding their flocks by night . . .

Tears moistened Lizzie's lashes, because she knew she was dreaming. Knew she wasn't on the Triple M, where she belonged, but trapped in a stranded train on a high, treacherous ridge.

The smell of coffee was real, though. That heartened her. Gave her the strength to open her eyes.

Her hair must have looked a sight, that was her immediate thought, and she needed to go outside. Her gaze found Morgan first, like a compass needle swinging north. He stood near the stove, looking rumpled from sleep, pouring coffee into a mug.

He crossed to her, handed her the cup.

The small courtesy seemed profound to Lizzie, rather than mundane.

"Today," she said, "is Christmas Eve."

"So it is," Morgan agreed, smiling wanly.

Whitley, resting with his broken leg propped on the bench seat, caught her eye. "Good morning, Lizziebet," he said.

She gave a little nod of acknowledgment, embarrassed by the nickname, and sipped at her coffee.

Evidently, Whitley's apology the day before had been a sincere one. He was on his best behavior. She discovered that she did not have an opinion on that, one way or the other.

"Where is Mr. Christian?" she asked Morgan, having scanned the company and noticed he was missing. The caboose was chilly, despite the efforts of the little stove. "Has he gone looking for firewood?"

A glance passed between Morgan and Whitley. Whitley raised both eyebrows, but didn't speak.

"He's on his way to Stone Creek," Morgan said, sounding resigned.

Lizzie sat up straighter, nearly spilling her coffee. "*Stone Creek?* That's miles from here—" She paused, confounded. "And you just *let him go?*"

Whitley finally deigned to contribute to the conversation. "He left before Dr. Shane woke up, Lizzie. And his mind was made up. Nobody could have stopped him."

Lizzie absorbed that. She thought of the tinkling music box and the tins of goose liver pâté and wondered if any of them would ever see Mr. Christian again.

"I'm going forward to the engine, for coal," Morgan said, taking up a bucket.

Lizzie thought of the conductor and engineer, lying frozen where they'd died. She thought of Mr. Christian, bravely making his way through snow that would be up to his waist in some places, over his head in others. The last, tattered joy of her Christmas dream faded away.

She simply nodded, and concentrated on drinking her coffee.

"Lizzie," Whitley said, when Morgan had gone, "come and sit here beside me."

The others were still sleeping. After a moment's hesitation, Lizzie crossed the caboose to join Whitley.

"Have you forgiven me?" Whitley asked, very quietly. His hazel eyes glowed with earnest affection; he really *was* a good person, Lizzie knew.

"I guess you were just scared," she said.

"I acted like a fool," Whitley told her.

Lizzie said nothing.

Shyly he took her hand. Squeezed it. "Now I've got to start the courtship all over again, don't I? I've botched things that badly."

"C-courtship?" Lizzie had looked forward to Whitley's proposal for months, dreamed of it, rehearsed the experience in her imagination, practiced her response. How many, many ways there were to say "yes." Now, something had changed, forever, and she knew it had far more to do with meeting Dr. Morgan Shane than anything Whitley had said or done since the avalanche. It wouldn't be fair, or kind, to pretend otherwise.

"Tell me I haven't lost you for good, Lizzie," Whitley said, tightening his grip on her hand as he read her face. "Please."

Just then, John Brennan began to cough so violently that Lizzie bolted off the seat and rushed across the caboose to help him sit up. The fit eased a little, but Lizzie felt desperately helpless, standing there patting the man's back while he struggled to breathe.

Whitley, meanwhile, got to his feet and stumped over to offer his flask. "It's just water," he said, when Lizzie looked at it askance, recalling all the whiskey he'd consumed from the vessel earlier.

She took the flask, opened it, held it to John's gray lips until he'd taken a few sips. After several tense moments, he seemed nominally better. Lizzie tested his forehead for fever, using the back of her hand as she'd seen Lorelei do so many times, and found it blazing hot.

Despair threatened Lizzie again. She swayed slightly on her feet, and Whitley caught hold of her arm just as Morgan returned, on a rush of cold wind, lugging a scuttle full of coal.

Time seemed to stop, just for a moment, as abruptly as the train had stopped when the avalanche struck.

Morgan carried the coal to the stove, crouched and tossed a few handfuls in on top of the last of the dry firewood.

Then the children woke up, and baby Nellie Anne began to wail for her breakfast. Whitley made his slow way back to the other side of the caboose, lowered himself onto the seat. Lizzie performed what ablutions she could, brushing her hair and pinning it up again, then grooming Ellen's hair, too. Mrs. Thaddings took Woodrow out of his cage so he could perch on her shoulder, ruffling his feathers and muttering bird prattle.

"Where's Mr. Christmas?" Jack asked, very seriously, as they all made a breakfast of leftover soup, crackers and goose liver pâté. Mrs. Halifax, clearly regaining her strength, had melted snow to wash her children's hands and faces, and they looked scrubbed and damp. "He said he'd teach me and Ellen to play five-card stud."

"He'll do no such thing," Mrs. Halifax said, but she smiled. Then she turned questioningly to Morgan. "Where *is* Mr. Christian?" she asked.

"He's making for Stone Creek," Whitley said, before Morgan could reply. "He should have stayed here."

Both Lizzie and Morgan gave him ironic looks—he'd broken his leg on a similar errand, after all—and he subsided, at least briefly.

Lizzie glanced at the windows overlooking the broad valley, hundreds of feet below the train's precarious perch on the mountainside. "At least the snow has stopped," she mused. "The traveling won't be any easier, but he'll be able to see where he's going."

Once the improvised meal was over, time seemed to crawl.

Mrs. Thaddings introduced Ellen and Jack to Woodrow, and they stared at him in fascination.

"If he was a homing pigeon," Ellen observed, bright child that she was, "he could go for help."

"We might have to eat him," Jack said solemnly, "if we run out of food."

Mr. Thaddings, who hadn't said much up until then, chuckled and shook his head. "He'd be pretty stringy," he told the boy.

"Stringy," Woodrow affirmed, spreading his wings and squawking once for emphasis.

Amused, Lizzie busied herself tending to John Brennan, while Morgan paced the center of the car and Mrs. Halifax discreetly nursed the baby, her back to everyone. Presently, when Woodrow retired to his cage for a nap, Jack and Ellen shyly approached Whitley, and sat themselves on either side of him.

He sighed, met Lizzie's gaze for a long moment, then flipped back to the front of the book he'd nearly finished, and began reading aloud. " 'It was the best of times—' "

And so the morning passed.

At midafternoon, a knock sounded at the door of the caboose.

Hope surged in Lizzie's heart—her father and uncles had come at last—but even before she opened the door, she knew they wouldn't have bothered to knock. They'd have busted down the door to get in.

Mr. Christian stood on the small platform, frost in his eyebrows, his whiskers, his lashes. He clutched a very small pine tree in one hand and gazed into

Lizzie's face without apparent recognition, more statue than man.

Morgan immediately moved her aside, took hold of the peddler by the arms, and pulled him in out of the cold.

"Tracks are blocked," Mr. Christian said woodenly, as Morgan took the tree from him and set it aside. "I had to turn back—"

Morgan began peeling off the man's coat, which appeared to be frozen and made a crackling sound as the fabric bent. Mr. Thaddings helped with the task, while Mrs. Thaddings rushed to fill a mug with coffee. Mr. Christian still seemed baffled, as though surprised to find himself where he was. Perhaps he wondered if he was in the caboose at all, or in the midst of some cold-induced reverie.

"Frostbite," Morgan said, examining the peddler's hands. "Lizzie, get me snow. Lots of snow."

Confounded, Lizzie obeyed just the same. She hurried out, filled the front of her skirt with as much snow as she could carry, returned to find that Morgan had settled Mr. Christian on the bench seat, as far from the stove as possible. She watched as Morgan took the snow she'd brought in, packed it around the peddler's hands and feet.

The process was repeated several more times, though when Mr. Thaddings saw that Lizzie's dress was wet, he took over the task, using the coal scuttle.

Mr. Christian lay on the train seat, shivering,

wearing only his long johns by then, staring mutely up at the roof of the car. He still did not seem precisely certain where he was, or what was happening to him, and Lizzie counted that as a mercy. She was relieved when Morgan finally gave the poor man an injection of morphine and stopped packing his extremities in snow.

"The children," Mr. Christian murmured once. "The children ought to have some kind of Christmas."

Tears scalded Lizzie's eyes. She had to turn away, and while Morgan was monitoring the patient's heartbeat, she sneaked out of the car, unnoticed by everyone but Whitley.

He started to raise an alarm, but at one pleading glance from Lizzie, he changed his mind.

She made her way to the baggage car and, after some lugging and maneuvering, began opening trunks until she'd found what she sought. Her fine woolen coat, the paint set she'd brought all this way to give to John Henry, shawls and stockings. A pipe she'd bought for her father. A book for her grandfather. A pocket watch she'd intended to give to Whitley. Next, she looted Whitley's trunk, helped herself to his heavy overcoat, more stockings and warm underwear. When a tiny velvet box toppled from the pocket of the coat, Lizzie's heart nearly stopped.

She bent, picked up the box, opened it slowly. A shining diamond ring winked inside. More tears came; so Whitley *had* intended to propose marriage over the holidays. Lizzie tucked her old dreams inside that box with the ring, closed it, set it carefully back in Whitley's trunk.

When she'd taken a few moments to recover, she bundled the things she'd gathered into Whitley's coat and made her way outside again, along the side of the train, into the caboose.

Her return, like her departure, caused no particular stir.

She set her burden aside and went to stand in front of the stove, trying to dry the front of her dress. John Brennan was already down with pneumonia, Whitley's leg was in splints, Mrs. Halifax sported a sling, and now poor Mr. Christian was nearly dead of frostbite. It wouldn't do if she added to their problems by taking sick herself.

Everyone settled into sort of a stupor after that.

Lizzie, now dry, turned to gaze out the windows. The sun was setting, and there was no sign of an approaching rescue party. She drew a deep breath.

It was still Christmas Eve, whatever the circumstances, and Lizzie was determined to celebrate in some way.

Soon the sky was peppered with stars, each one shining as brightly as the diamond ring Whitley had meant to place on her finger. The snow glittered, deep and pristine, under those spilling stars, and the scent of the little pine tree Mr. Christian had somehow cut and brought back spiced the air.

Morgan looted the freight car again, and returned with a stack of new blankets and the spectacular Christmas ham they'd all agreed not to eat, just the day before. He fetched more coal and built up the fire, and they feasted—even John Brennan and Mr. Christian managed a few bites.

As the moon rose, spilling shimmering silver over the snow, Morgan stuck the trunk of the tiny tree between the slats of Mr. Christian's empty crate, and Whitley donated his watch chain for a decoration. Lizzie contributed several hair ribbons from her handbag, along with a small mirror that seemed to catch the starlight. Mrs. Thaddings contributed her ear bobs.

They sang, Lizzie starting first, Mrs. Halifax picking up the words next, her voice faltering, then John and Whitley and the children. Even Woodrow joined in.

" 'O little town of Bethlehem, how still we see thee lie . . .' "

"We ain't gettin' our oranges," Jack announced stoically, as his mother tucked him and Ellen into the quilt bed, after many more carols had been sung. "There's no stockings to hang, and St. Nicholas won't find us way out here."

Ellen gazed at the little tree as though it were the most splendid thing she'd ever set eyes on. "It's Christmas, just the same," she said. "And that tree is right pretty. Mr. Christmas went to a lot of trouble to bring it back for us, too."

Jack sighed and closed his eyes.

Ellen gazed at the tree until she fell asleep.

Morgan moved back and forth between John Brennan and Mr. Christian. He'd given Whitley more laudanum after supper, when the pain in his injured leg had contorted his face and brought out a sheen of sweat across his forehead. Mr. and Mrs. Thaddings, having settled Woodrow down for the night, read from a worn Bible.

Watching them, Lizzie marveled at their calm acceptance. It seemed that, as long as they were together, they could face anything. She knew so little about the couple, and yet it would be obvious to anyone who looked that the marriage was a refuge for them both.

She wanted to be like them. To get old with someone, to live out an unfurling ribbon of years, as they had.

Presently, she turned to Morgan.

"I thought they'd come," Lizzie confided, very quietly. She was kneeling in front of the tree by then, breathing in the scent of it, remembering so many things. "I thought my family would come."

Morgan moved to sit cross-legged beside her. He said nothing at all, but simply listened.

A tear slipped down Lizzie's cheek. She dashed it away with the back of one hand. Straightened her spine.

"Maybe in the morning," she said.

"Maybe," Morgan agreed, gently gruff.

She got to her feet, retrieved the bundle she'd brought from the baggage car earlier. She folded Whitley's expensive overcoat neatly, placed it beneath the tree. John Henry's paint set went next, and then the pocket watch. Her beautiful velvet-collared coat found its way under the tree, too, and so did the pipe and the book and a few other things, as well.

She sat back on her heels when she'd finished arranging the gifts. Was surprised when Morgan reached out and took her hand.

"Lizzie McKettrick," he said, "you are something."

She bit her lower lip. Glanced in Whitley's direction to make certain he was asleep. He seemed to be, but he might have been "playing possum," to use one of her grandfather's favorite terms.

"He's going to ask me to marry him," she said, without intending to speak at all.

Morgan was silent for a long moment. Then he replied, "And you'll say yes."

She shook her head, unable to look directly at Morgan.

"Why not?" Morgan asked, his voice pitched low. It seemed intimate, their talking in the semidarkness, now that the lamp had been extinguished, the way her papa and Lorelei so often did, late at night, when they were alone in the kitchen, with the stove-fire banked low and the savory smell of supper still lingering in the air.

"Because it wouldn't be right," Lizzie said. "For

Whitley or for me. He's a good man, Morgan. He really is. He deserves a wife who loves him."

Morgan didn't answer. Not right away, at least. "These are trying circumstances, Lizzie—for all of us. Don't make any hasty decisions. You'll have a long time to regret it if you make the wrong ones."

Again, Lizzie glanced in Whitley's direction, then down at her hands, knotted atop the fabric of her ruined skirts. "Maybe I'm not cut out to be married anyhow," she ventured. "Some people aren't, you know."

She felt his smile, rather than saw it. "It would be a waste, Lizzie, if you didn't marry. But I agree that you're better off single than tied to the wrong man."

"My pupils," Lizzie mused. "They'll be my children." Even as she said the words, a soft sorrow tugged at her heart. She so wanted babies of her own, sons and daughters, bringing the kind of rowdy, chaotic joy swelling the walls of the houses on the Triple M.

"Will they be enough, Lizzie?" Morgan asked, after a lengthy silence. "Your pupils, I mean?"

"I don't know," she answered sadly.

Morgan squeezed her hand again. "You have time, Lizzie. You're a beautiful woman. If you and Whitley can't come to terms, you'll surely meet someone else."

Lizzie feared she'd already met that "someone else," and he was Morgan. Normally a confident person, she suddenly felt out of her depth. The

McKettricks were certainly prominent, and they were wealthy, but they lived in ranch houses, not mansions. Nobody dressed for dinner, or employed servants, or rode in fancy carriages, as Morgan's people surely had. She'd attended Miss Ridgley's, where she'd learned which fork to use with which course of a meal, how to embroider and entertain, and after that she'd gone to San Francisco Normal School. Morgan had studied medicine abroad. Estranged from his mother or not, he would be at home in high society, while Lizzie would be considered a frontier bumpkin at worst, one of the nouveaux riches at best.

"Lizzie?" Morgan prompted, when she didn't reply to his comment.

"I was just wondering why you'd want to live and work in a place like Indian Rock, instead of Chicago or New York or Philadelphia or Boston," she said. "Don't you miss . . . well . . . all the things there are to *do* in places like that?"

"Such as?"

"Concerts. Art museums. Stores so big you have to climb stairs to see everything they sell."

Morgan chuckled. "Do *you* miss concerts and museums and shopping, Lizzie?"

"No," she said. "San Francisco is beautiful—I really enjoyed being there. I made a lot of friends at school. But there were times when I was so homesick, I wasn't sure I could stand it."

Morgan caressed her cheek with the backs of his

knuckles, his touch so gentle that a hot shiver went through her. "I guess I'm homesick, too," he said, "but in a different way. The home I want is the one I never had—the one I'm hoping to find in Indian Rock."

Lizzie's throat thickened. It was only too easy to picture Morgan as a small child, having Christmas dinner in the kitchen of some yawning mausoleum of a house, with only the family cook for company. On the other hand, things would be different in Indian Rock—once word got around town that the new doctor didn't have a wife, the scheming and flirtations would begin. Meals would be cooked and brought to his door in baskets. He'd be invited to Sunday suppers, and unmarried women for miles around would suddenly develop delicate ailments requiring the immediate attention of the attractive new physician.

Thinking of it made Lizzie give a very unladylike snort.

In the moonlight, she saw Morgan's right eyebrow rise slightly, and a smile played at one corner of his mouth. "Now, what accounts for *that* reaction, Lizzie McKettrick?" he asked.

She loved it when he called her by her full name, though she could not have said why. But she was mightily embarrassed that she'd snorted in front of him, like an old horse nickering for oats. "You won't be single long," she said. "Once you get to Indian Rock, I mean."

She regretted the statement instantly; it revealed too much. Like a contentious colt, it had bolted from the place she contained such things and kicked up a fuss inside Lizzie.

Again, that crooked little smile from Morgan. "I think I'd like to be married," he mused, surprising her yet again; she'd *thought* she was getting used to his blunt way of speaking. "A lovely wife. A passel of children. It all sounds very good to me right now, but maybe I'm just being sentimental."

For some reason she could not define, Lizzie wanted to cry. And it wasn't because she was far from home on Christmas Eve, or because she knew she would have to turn down Whitley's proposal and he would be hurt and disappointed, or even because all their lives were in danger.

Not trusting herself to speak, or govern what she said if she made the attempt, Lizzie remained silent.

Morgan brushed her cheek with the tips of his fingers. "Get some sleep," he counseled. "Tomorrow's Christmas."

Tomorrow's Christmas. Lizzie found that hard to credit, even with the little tree and the presents so carefully arranged beneath it. She nodded, and she was about to get to her feet when, with no warning at all, Morgan suddenly caught her face between his hands and placed the lightest, sweetest kiss imaginable on her mouth.

A jolt shot through Lizzie; she might have captured liquid lightning in a metal cup, like fresh spring rain, and swigged it down. She knew Morgan felt her trembling before he lowered his hands from her face to take hers and help her to her feet.

"Good night, Lizzie McKettrick," he said gruffly. "And a happy Christmas."

She found a place to lie down on one of the long bench seats, never dreaming that she'd sleep. Her heart leaped and frolicked like a circus performer on a trampoline, and she could still feel Morgan's brief, innocent kiss tingling on her lips.

To distract herself from all the contradictory feelings Morgan had aroused in her, she imagined herself at home on the Triple M. She stood for a few moments in the familiar kitchen, lamp-lit and warm from the stove, and saw her papa and Lorelei sitting in their usual places at the table, though they did not seem to see her.

Mentally, she climbed the back stairway, made her way first to the room John Henry, Gabriel and Doss shared. They were all sound asleep in their beds, fair hair tousled on the pillows and flecked with hay from the customary Christmas Eve visit to the barn, and each one had hung a stocking from a hook on the wall, in anticipation of St. Nicholas's arrival. The stockings were still limp and empty—Lorelei would fill them later, when she was sure they wouldn't awaken. Rock candy. Toy whistles. Perhaps small wooden animals, hand carved by Papa, out in the wood shop.

The scene was achingly real to Lizzie—it made her

eyes sting and her throat ache so fiercely that she put a hand to it. As she stared down at her brothers, drinking in the sight of them, John Henry opened his eyes, looked directly at her.

"Where are you?" he asked, using his hands to sign the words he couldn't speak.

Lizzie signed back. "I'll be home soon."

John Henry's small hands flew. "Promise?"

"Promise," Lizzie confirmed.

And then the vision faded, leaving Lizzie longing to find it again.

As she settled her nerves, she was aware of Morgan moving about the caboose, probably checking his various patients: Mrs. Halifax with her injured arm, Whitley with his broken leg, the peddler, Mr. Christian, who'd nearly gotten himself frozen to death, and last of all poor John Brennan, struggling with pneumonia.

And over them all loomed the mountain, ominously silent.

Finally Lizzie slept.

Christmas.

It had never meant so much to Morgan as it did that night. He wanted to give Lizzie everything—trinkets, the finest silks and laces, and beyond those things . . . his heart. For a brief fraction of a moment, he actually wished he'd granted his mother's wishes and become a banker, instead of a doctor.

Annoyed with himself, he shoved both hands

through his hair, as he always did when he was frustrated—and that was often.

He concentrated on what he knew, taking care of the sick and injured, knowing full well that sleep would elude him.

John Brennan seemed marginally better.

Mrs. Halifax would be fine, once she'd gotten some real rest.

Mr. Thaddings was resting quietly, the bluish color gone from his lips.

Even Christian, the peddler, who had come dangerously close to dying, appeared to be rallying somewhat. He might lose a few toes, but otherwise, he'd probably be his old self soon.

Whitley Carson's leg would mend; he was young, healthy and strong. Unless he was the biggest fool who ever lived, he'd pursue Lizzie until she accepted his proposal, married him and bore his children. Maybe he was smart enough to know that a woman like Lizzie McKettrick came along about as often as the proverbial blue moon, and maybe he wasn't.

Morgan hoped devoutly for the latter.

If they got out of this situation alive, Morgan decided, and if Lizzie *didn't* change her mind about marrying Whitley, by some miracle, he would court her himself.

Did he love her?

He didn't know. He certainly admired her, respected her and, God knew, *wanted* her, and not just physically. She'd opened some whole new region in his soul, an actual landscape, golden with light. Should Lizzie refuse his suit, as she well might, he'd have that magical place to retreat into, for the rest of his life, and he'd find some sad solace there.

He shook his head. Such thoughts were utterly foreign to his nature. He was a realist; did not have a fanciful bone in his body. He was a doctor, not a poet. And yet Lizzie had changed him, and he knew the alteration was permanent.

The coffee was cold, and full of grounds, but he poured some anyway, and lifted it to his lips. Moved to the window side of the car to look out over the blue-white night. He sipped, pondering the irony of meeting Lizzie in this peculiar time and place.

And before he'd swallowed a second sip of coffee, he heard the deep, growling rumble overhead.

Chapter Six

The caboose shook violently, rousing Lizzie instantly from a shallow sleep. She sat bolt upright, the startled shouts of the others echoing in her ears, her heart in her throat, and waited for the railroad car to go tumbling over the side of the cliff.

It didn't.

There was a second great shudder, and then . . . stillness.

Was this what it was like to die?

She looked around, but the darkness was as

densely black as India ink. She might have been at the bottom of a coal mine at midnight, for all she could see.

"Morgan?" she called softly.

"I'm here," he assured her, from somewhere close by.

"What happened?" asked one of the children.

"How come it's so dark?" inquired the other, the words scrambling over those of the other child.

"Dark!" Woodrow fretted loudly. "Dark!"

"There's been another avalanche," Morgan said matter-of-factly, over Woodrow's continuing rant. "The snow must be blocking the windows, but we're still on the tracks, I think."

"Did the Christmas tree get ruint?" Lizzie identified the voice as Ellen's.

"Never mind the Christmas tree," Whitley said, sounding testy and shaken. "And will somebody shut that bird up?"

"Will somebody shut that bird up?" Woodrow repeated.

"How long will the air last?" John Brennan asked.

"I don't know," Morgan asked. "Everybody stay put. I'll see if I can get the door open to have a look. Maybe we can dig our way out."

"We could smother in here," Whitley said.

"Hush," Lizzie snapped. "We're not going to smother!"

"Stringy bird!" Woodrow prattled on. "Don't eat the bird!"

The baby began to cry, first tentatively, then with a full-lunged wail.

Mrs. Halifax sang to the infant, her soft voice quavering.

Mrs. Thaddings spoke tenderly to Woodrow.

A match was struck, lamplight flared, feeble against the terrible darkness. Morgan stood holding the lantern, a man woven of shadows. The incongruous thought came to Lizzie that he needed a shave.

Snow covered the windows on both sides of the car now, and it was clear that Morgan had been unable to force the door open. They were effectively buried alive.

Remarkably, the forlorn little Christmas tree still stood, the gifts undisturbed beneath it.

"Look!" Ellen cried, nudging a blinking Jack and pointing to the spectacle. "St. Nicholas came!"

Lizzie's gaze locked with Morgan's. Something unspoken passed between them, and Morgan nodded.

Lizzie worked up a cheerful smile. "And there are presents for everyone," she said, making her way to the tree. She took her prized coat up first, handed it to Mrs. Halifax. "For you," she said. She gave John Henry's paint set to Ellen and Jack, and Whitley's hand-tailored overcoat went to John Brennan, the pipe she'd bought for her father to Mr. Christian. Whitley got the book, and Morgan the pocket watch. She gave Mr. and Mrs. Thaddings a small box of hand-dipped chocolates from a shop in San Francisco, specially chosen for Lorelei.

"What about you?" Ellen asked, staring first at the paint set and then at Lizzie. "Isn't there something for you, Miss Lizzie?"

For the first time since he'd returned to the railroad car, clutching that little tree, Mr. Christian spoke a coherent sentence. "Why, St. Nicholas meant the music box for Lizzie," he said weakly.

Ellen relaxed, much to Lizzie's relief, and set to examining the paints and brushes and special paper she and Jack were to share. She wouldn't accept the music box, of course, as generous as Mr. Christian was to offer it—it had belonged to his late wife, after all. It was an heirloom.

They couldn't build a fire, for fear the chimney was covered by a deep layer of snow, and the chill set in pretty quickly. If they were going to die, Lizzie decided, they would die in good spirits.

She squared her shoulders and lifted her chin, but before she could speak, she heard the first, faint clank, and then another.

"Listen!" she said, shushing everyone.

Another clank, and then another—metal, striking metal. Shovels? Distant and faint, perhaps up the line of cars a ways, toward the engine.

"They're here," Lizzie whispered. "They're here!"

Everyone looked up, as though expecting their rescuers to descend through the roof.

Time seemed to stop.

Clank, clank, clank.

And then—some minutes later—footsteps on the metal roof of the caboose, a muffled voice.

Her papa's voice.

"Lizzie!" Holt McKettrick called.

"In here, Papa!" Lizzie cried, on a joyous sob. "In the caboose!"

She heard him speak to the others—her uncles and perhaps even her grandfather. The clanking commenced in earnest then, and the voices became clearer.

"Lizzie?" Her papa again. "Hold on, sweetheart."

The door Morgan had been unable to open earlier jostled on its hinges, then creaked with an ear-splitting squeal. Holt McKettrick gave a wrench from outside, and then he was there, filling the chasm.

Big. Strong. So handsome he made Lizzie's heart swell with pride and gladness. Holt McKettrick would have moved heaven and earth, if he had to, for his daughter, for a train full of strangers.

Lizzie flew to him.

He scooped her up into his arms, clean off her feet, and kissed her hard on top of the head. She felt the warmth of his tears in her hair. "Thank God," he murmured. *"Thank God."*

She clung, crying freely now, not even trying to hold back the sobs of joy rising from the very core of her being. "Papa . . . Papa!"

"Hush," Holt said gruffly. "You're all right now, girl."

Behind him, she saw her uncles enter—Rafe then Kade then Jeb. Then another man, someone Lizzie didn't recognize.

"Pa!" Ellen and Jack screamed in unison, rushing to be enfolded in the tall, lean cowboy's waiting arms. Over their heads he exchanged a look of reverent gratitude with Mrs. Halifax, who was holding the baby so tightly that it struggled in her embrace. Tears slipped down her face.

Lizzie finally recovered a modicum of composure when Holt set her back on her feet. She gulped, looking up at him. "I knew you'd come," she said.

Holt grinned. "Of course we came," he replied. "We couldn't have had Christmas without our Lizzie."

"S-some of the others are hurt," Lizzie said, remembering suddenly, feeling some chagrin that, in her excitement, she'd forgotten them.

Her uncles were already assessing the situation.

"We'd better get out of here quick, Holt," Rafe said, with an upward glance. He was a big man, burly and dark-haired, his eyes the intense blue of a chambray work shirt.

Kade, meanwhile, greeted Morgan with a handshake. "Hell of a welcome to Indian Rock," he said, as Lizzie drank in the sight of him—well built, with chestnut hair and a quiet manner. He gave her a wink.

Morgan looked solemn—and completely exhausted. "The engineer and the conductor didn't make it," he told Kade. "They're in the locomotive."

Kade nodded grimly. "We'll have to come back for them later," he said. "Along with any trunks or the like. Rafe's right. We'd best get while the getting is good."

After that, things happened fast, and Lizzie experienced it all through a numbing haze, shimmering silvery at the edges. They'd brought a large, flat-bed sleigh, as Lizzie had expected they would, piled with loose straw and drawn by four gigantic plow horses. There were blankets and bear hides, too, to keep the travelers warm, and flasks filled with strong spirits. Farther along the tracks, her father told her, half the hands from the Triple M waited, having set up camp the night before, when they'd all had to stop because of the darkness and the weather.

Lizzie was bundled, like a child, in quilts she recognized from home, and her uncle Jeb, the youngest McKettrick brother, fair-haired and agile, carried her to the sleigh. She settled into a sort of dizzy stupor, the sweet scent of the fresh straw lulling her further.

"You're safe now, Lizzie-bet," Jeb told her, his azure eyes glistening suspiciously. "Pa kicked up some kind of fuss when we wouldn't let him come along to find you. Too hard on his heart, Concepcion said. We had to hogtie him and throw him in jail, and we could still hear him bellowing five miles out of town."

Lizzie smiled at the image of her proud grandfather behind bars. He'd be prowling like a caged mountain lion, furious that they'd left him behind. "There'll be the devil to pay when you let him out," she warned.

Jeb chuckled, ran the sleeve of his wool-lined leather coat across his eyes. "We're counting on you to put in a good word for us," he said, tucking straw in around her before turning to go back and help bring out the others.

When they had all been rescued, and placed securely on the back of the heavy sled, Holt took the reins and shouted to the team. Kade and Jeb rode mules, as did Mr. Halifax.

The going was slow, the snow being so deep, and it was precarious. Lizzie drifted in and out of her hazy reverie, aware of Whitley nearby, and Morgan at a little distance.

Considerable time passed before they reached the camp Holt had mentioned. Cowboys greeted them with hot coffee and good cheer, and they lingered awhile, in a broad, snowy clearing under a copse of bare-limbed oak trees, safe from the possibility of another avalanche.

It was past nightfall when they reached Indian Rock.

A soft snow was falling, church bells rang, and it seemed the whole town had turned out to greet the Christmas travelers. Lorelei rushed to Lizzie, knelt on the bed of the sleigh, and pulled her into her arms.

"Lizzie," she whispered, over and over again. "Oh, Lizzie!"

Next, Lizzie saw her grandfather, tall and fierce-faced, his thick white hair askew because he'd been thrusting his fingers through it. His gaze swept over his sons, daring any one of them to interfere, then he gathered Lizzie right up and carried her inside the Arizona Hotel.

The lobby was blessedly warm, and alight with glowing lamps.

There were people everywhere.

"Lizzie-bet," Angus McKettrick said, "you like to scared me to death when your train didn't turn up on time."

Lizzie rested her head against his strong shoulder. "I'm sorry, Grampa," she said. Then she looked up into his face. "I reckon you're pretty mad at Papa and Kade and Rafe and Jeb," she ventured. "For locking you up, I mean."

"I'll have their hides for it," Angus vowed, and though his voice was rough as sandpaper, Lizzie heard the tenderness in it. He loved his four sons deeply, and probably understood that they'd only been trying to protect him by throwing him in the hoosegow. "Right now, Lizzie-girl, all I care about is that you're safe. Soon as you've rested up, we'll all head home to the Triple M."

"I guess I missed Christmas," Lizzie said.

Angus carried her up the stairs and into a waiting room. He laid her gently on the bed, and stepped back to let Lorelei attend to her. Only then did he reply, "You didn't miss Christmas. We held it for you."

"Leave us alone, Angus," Lorelei said quietly. "I need to get Lizzie out of these wet, cold clothes and into something warm and dry."

Angus clenched his jaw, then inclined his head to Lizzie in reluctant farewell before leaving the room and closing the door softly behind him.

"What happened out there?" Lorelei asked, as she deftly undid the buttons on Lizzie's shoes.

"There was an avalanche," Lizzie said. The warmth of the room made her skin burn, and she wondered, briefly, if she'd been frostbitten. If she'd lose fingers and toes or maybe an ear. Tears scalded her eyes. She was *alive,* that was what mattered. And she was home—or almost home. "I didn't let myself think for one moment that Papa and the others wouldn't come for us." Her conscience stirred. "Well," she added, "maybe there were a *few* moments—"

Lorelei smiled gently, continuing to peel away Lizzie's clothes, then dressing her again in a long flannel nightgown. "You were McKettrick tough," Lorelei said, when she'd pulled the bedcovers up to Lizzie's chin. "We're all very proud of you, Lizzie."

"The others—Morgan, Whitley . . . the children . . . ?"

"They're all being taken care of, sweetheart. Don't worry."

Lizzie closed her eyes, sighed. "I hope I'm not dreaming," she said "You're really here, aren't you, Lorelei? You and Papa and Grampa—?"

"Rest, Lizzie," Lorelei said, with tears in her voice.

"It's not a dream. You're back home in Indian Rock, with your family around you."

She recalled the Thaddingses and how they expected to find Miss Clarinda Adams running a dressmaker's shop, not a high-toned brothel. Would Miss Adams take them in, Mr. and Mrs. Thaddings and Woodrow? Or would they refuse, in their inevitable shock, to accept hospitality from the town madam?

Where would they go, either way? Lizzie knew very little about them, but she had discerned that they weren't rich.

"There's an older couple—they have a bird—they think Clarinda Adams makes dresses for a living—"

Lorelei smiled, patting Lizzie's hand. "Clarinda's moved on," she said. "Married one of her clients and high-tailed it back east three months ago."

"But Mr. and Mrs. Thaddings—they expected to stay with her. . . ."

"Everyone will be taken care of, Lizzie, so stop worrying. Right now, you need to rest."

"There's a bird—"

"Hush," Lorelei said, kissing Lizzie's forehead. "I'll make sure the Thaddingses *and* their bird find lodging."

Lizzie sighed again and slept.

Morgan assessed his new quarters. The town had built on to the hotel, providing him with a small office and examination room and living space behind that. The place was well furnished and well supplied. He found coffee on the shelf above the small stove and put some on to brew.

His bed was within kicking distance, narrow and made up with clean blankets, obviously secondhand. There was a bathtub, too, a great, incongruous thing served by a complicated system of exposed pipes, equally close, and with a copper hot water tank attached to the wall above it.

He smiled to himself. If only his mother could see him now.

Morgan lit the gas jet under the boiler on the hot water tank—it would take a while to heat—and put coffee on to brew while he waited. Finally he filled the tub with water, steaming gloriously. His clothes and other belongings were still on the train, out there on the mountainside, but thanks to the McKettricks, he'd been provided with a change of clothes, shaving gear, soap and a tall bottle of whiskey.

After he poured coffee into a chipped cup, also donated no doubt, and then added a generous dollop of whiskey for good measure, he stripped and lowered himself into the tub.

The bath was bliss, and so was the whiskey-laced coffee. But the best thing was knowing Lizzie was all right, safe upstairs, being cared for by her stepmother.

John Brennan's family had been right there to greet him as soon as they arrived, and two of the townsmen had carried him, blanket-wrapped and half-delirious, toward the mercantile. If John made it through the night, Morgan figured he'd have a good chance of surviving.

Whitley Carson was resting in one of the hotel rooms, as were the Halifaxes, the Thaddingses and Woodrow.

Morgan hadn't seen where the peddler was taken, but he assumed he'd been gathered up, too, by kinfolks or friends. For the time being, Morgan could allow himself to simply be a very relieved, very tired man, not a doctor.

He finished the coffee and soaked until the water began to cool, then hastily shaved, scrubbed and got out of the tub. Dressed in his borrowed clothes, he headed for the lobby. The place was so crowded he'd have sworn somebody was throwing a party.

After a few moments, he realized his first impression had been right. The entire town seemed to be present, hoisting a glass, celebrating that the lost had been found. Kade caught his eye and beckoned, and Morgan followed him through the cheerful throng into the hotel dining room.

"Figured you'd be hungry for hot food," McKettrick said.

Morgan *was* hungry, though he hadn't realized it until that moment. His stomach grumbled loudly, and he sat down at one of the tables next to the window, looking out at the Christmas-card snowfall.

A waitress appeared, and Kade, seated across from

him, ordered for them both. There was no one else in the dining room.

"Thanks," Morgan said.

McKettrick raised one eyebrow, but didn't speak.

"For coming for us," Morgan clarified. "Lizzie said you would. I don't think she ever doubted it—but I wasn't so sure."

Kade smiled fondly at the mention of Lizzie's name. "If there's one of us missing from the supper table," he said, "the rest will turn the whole countryside on its top to find them."

"It must be nice to be part of a family like that," Morgan said, without really meaning to. He didn't feel sorry for himself, and he didn't want to give the impression that he did.

"It has its finer moments," Kade answered mildly. "I take it you don't come from a big outfit like ours?"

"There's just me," Morgan replied. "That peddler—Mr. Christian—did somebody come to meet him?"

Kade frowned. "Who?"

The waitress returned with hot bread, a butter dish and two cups of coffee, all balanced on a tray.

Morgan didn't answer until she'd gone again.

"Mr. Christian. An older man, a peddler with a sample case."

Kade shook his head. "I don't recall anybody fitting that description," he said. "There was you and Lizzie, the Halifaxes, the soldier, an elderly pair with a bird and the yahoo with the broken leg."

Morgan started to rise from his chair, certain the

old peddler must have been left behind by mistake. Or maybe he'd fallen off the sleigh, somewhere along the way, and nobody had noticed—

"Sit down," Kade said. "We got everybody off that train. Everybody who was still alive, anyway."

Morgan sank back into his chair, befuddled. "But there has to be some kind of mistake. There was an old man—ask Lizzie—ask any of the others—"

"I'll do that, if it makes you happy," Kade allowed. "But we got everybody there was to get."

The food came. Fried chicken, mashed potatoes swimming in gravy, green beans cooked with onions and bacon. It was a feast, and Morgan was so desperately hungry that he practically dove into his plate. He was done-in, he told himself. Not thinking straight. In the morning, after a good night's sleep, he'd make sense of the matter of Mr. Christmas, as the children had called him.

They'd lighted the candles on the tree for him, and made him up a nice bed on the settee, there in the fine apartments above the mercantile, and his wife and boy were staying close, while the in-laws hovered in the distance. There was good food cooking, and a fire blazing on the hearth, and John Brennan figured he'd died for sure and gone straight to heaven.

"St. Nicholas *did too* come," Jack told his smilingly skeptical father. "He brought a paint set for Ellen and me."

"Did he now?" Ben Halifax asked his son. Mama, Ellen and the baby were all sleeping, cozied up in the same hotel bed. Ben and Jack would share the other, and, in the morning, if the weather was good and everybody was up to the trip, they'd all head out to the Triple M, where they'd be staying on, not just passing through. "I guess he must have been in two places at once, then, because he filled some stockings out at the ranch, too."

Jack widened his eyes. He'd had supper, and he knew he ought to be in bed asleep, like his mama and sisters, but he was just plain too excited. "But me and Ellen wasn't there to hang any stockings," he argued.

"I hung them up for you," his father said. "And darned if I didn't wake up this morning and find those old work socks just a-bulging with presents."

Jack blinked, wonderstruck. "I guess if anybody could be in two places at once," he said with certainty, "it would be St. Nicholas who done it."

Ben laughed, ruffled the boy's hair. His eyes glistened, and if Jack hadn't known better, he'd have bet his pa was crying. "It's Christmas," Ben said, his voice sounding all scrapey and rough. "The time when miracles happen."

"What's a miracle?" Jack asked, puzzled.

"It's having you and your ma and your sisters right here with me, where you belong," Ben answered. Then he did something Jack couldn't remember him ever doing before. He lifted Jack onto his lap, held him real tight, and kissed him on top of the head. "Yesiree, that's all the miracle I need."

Zebulon Thaddings bent to strike a match to the fire laid in the hearth of the sumptuously decorated parlor. The lamps all had painted globes, the rugs were foreign, the furniture plentiful and fussy, and there were naked people cavorting in the paintings on the walls.

"Your sister has done well, for a dressmaker," he told Marietta, who was gazing about with an expression of troubled wonder on her dear face. In point of fact, he hadn't wanted to make this journey in the first place, since he'd known all along, even if his wife hadn't, how Clarinda had been able to afford the fine jewelry and exquisite clothing she'd worn when she visited them in Phoenix. There simply hadn't been any other possible explanation.

Zebulon had lost his job running an Indian school, and with it, of course, the minuscule salary and the tiny house provided for the headmaster and his wife. They were destitute. The plain and difficult truth was that they had hoped Clarinda would take them in, along with Woodrow, not just welcome them for a holiday visit.

They'd had nowhere else to go, and Zebulon had used the last few dollars he had, to pay for their train fare to Indian Rock.

Now they were basically squatting in Clarinda's grand house. God only knew where they would go next, but for the time being, at least, they had a roof over their heads, a bed to sleep in, and a pantry stocked with foodstuffs.

Woodrow, provided with a fresh supply of birdseed by a kindly shopkeeper, sat in his shiny cage, looking around.

"Why are all these people . . . naked?" Marietta fretted, wringing her hands a little as she took in the large and scandalous painting above the fireplace. Bare-fleshed men and women lay about a forest, some of them intertwined, eating grapes, sipping from elaborate chalices and generally looking swoony.

"Naked!" Woodrow exclaimed. "Naked as a jay-bird!"

Woodrow mostly repeated the words of others, but occasionally, like now, he added commentary of his own from his past repertoire. Zebulon had to smile.

Crossing to Marietta, the Turkish rug soft beneath the thin soles of his shoes, he embraced his wife. She'd been a true helpmeet over the years, never complaining about their near penury, never voicing her great disappointment that they hadn't been blessed with children of their own.

"Dearest," he said, after clearing his throat. "About Clarinda—"

Marietta looked up at him, tears gleaming in her gentle eyes. "She isn't a dressmaker, is she?"

Zebulon shook his head. "No," he answered.

"What are we going to do, Zebulon?"

Zebulon's own eyes burned. He blinked rapidly. "I don't know," he said.

"Perhaps Clarinda intends to return soon," Marietta speculated hopefully, brightening a little.

"Perhaps," Zebulon agreed, though doubtful.

"Hadn't we better send her a wire or write a letter? Someone in Indian Rock must have her address."

The scent of cigar smoke lingered in the air. Clarinda's possessions were all around, giving the strange impression that she'd merely left the room, not the territory.

"You ought to lie down and rest awhile, dear," Zebulon told Marietta. "I'll brew a nice pot of tea."

Marietta hesitated, then nodded. Gently raised, and a preacher's daughter into the bargain, she hadn't quite accepted the obvious—that her spirited younger sister ran a house of ill repute. She settled herself on the long, plush sofa facing the fireplace, and Zebulon covered her tenderly with a knitted afghan.

"Tea!" Woodrow chirped, as Zebulon left the room, headed for the massive kitchen. "Tea for two!"

When Lizzie opened her eyes, the room was full of snow-gleam, and her young brothers were standing next to her bed. Well, at least, John Henry was standing—Doss and Gabriel were jumping up and down on the foot of the mattress, shouting, "Wake up! Wake up!"

Lizzie laughed, used her elbows to push herself upright. After fluffing her pillows, she leaned back against them.

Lorelei appeared and whisked the younger boys away, both of them protesting vigorously. Was Lizzie going to sleep all day long? Wouldn't they *ever* get to go home and open their Christmas presents?

John Henry stayed behind, regarding Lizzie with solemn, thoughtful eyes.

She ruffled his hair.

"I saw you in our room," John Henry signed. "On Christmas Eve."

A shock went through Lizzie as she remembered her imagined visit home. "I was still on the train on Christmas Eve," she signed back.

John Henry shook his head, repeated, the motions of his small, deft hands insistent, "I *saw* you, Lizzie," he reiterated. "You were wearing a man's coat and your hair was all mussed up. You said not to worry, because you were coming home soon."

Lizzie blinked. Something tightened in her throat, making it impossible to speak.

The door of the hotel room opened, and her father came in. He sent John Henry downstairs to have breakfast with his brothers, and the child scampered to obey, but not before he cast one last, knowing look back at Lizzie.

Holt dragged a chair up alongside the bed. "Feeling better?" he asked.

Lizzie nodded.

"Lorelei's bringing up a tray. All your favorites. Sausage, hotcakes with lots of syrup, and tea."

He offered Lizzie his hand, and she took it. After swallowing, she managed to speak. "Morgan," she said. "Is he . . . is he all right?"

"He's fine," Holt answered with a slight frown. "I guess I figured you'd be more interested in the other one. According to young Mr. Carson, he means to set about claiming your hand in marriage, first chance he gets. Already asked for my permission to propose."

Lizzie's emotions must have shown clearly on her face, because her father's frown deepened. "What did you say?" she asked, almost in a whisper.

"I told him you were nineteen years old, and if you want to marry him, that's all right by me." Holt shifted in the hotel chair, which seemed almost too spindly to support his powerful frame. "Should I have said something different, Lizzie?"

A tear slipped down Lizzie's cheek. "I don't love Whitley, Papa. I thought I did—oh, I *really* thought I did—but when everything happened up there on the mountain—"

Holt leaned forward, folded his arms, rested them on his knees as he regarded his daughter. "It's the doctor you love, then," he said. "Morgan Shane."

"I wouldn't say I love him," Lizzie replied slowly, after some thought. "I don't know *what* I feel. He's strong and he's good and when people were hurt and sick, he forgot about himself and did what had to be done. On the other hand, he makes me so angry sometimes—"

Holt smiled. "I see. I assume Mr. Carson didn't comport himself in the same way?"

"No," Lizzie said. "But I suppose I could overlook that, if I wanted to. It's just that, when I met Morgan, everything changed."

"Well then, when the proposal comes, you'll have to turn it down."

"Couldn't you just—withdraw your permission? Tell Whitley you've changed your mind and he can't propose to me after all?"

Her father chuckled, shook his head. "It isn't like you to take the coward's way out," he said. "You brought that young fella all the way up here from California, intending to show him off to all of us and, I suspect, hoping he'd give you an engagement ring. You'll have to tell him the truth, Lizzie. However he might have behaved on that train, he deserves that much."

Lizzie sighed heavily and sank back onto her pillows. "You're right," she said dolefully.

Holt laughed. "It's nice to hear you admit that," he said, as Lorelei came in with the promised tray, and despite the prospect of refusing Whitley Carson's suit, Lizzie ate with a good appetite. She expected to remember that particular meal for the rest of her natural life, it was so delicious.

When her father had gone—there had been a thaw, and he, Rafe, Kade and Jeb were heading out to the ranch to feed livestock—Lorelei had a bathtub brought to the room and filled bucket by bucket with gloriously hot water. After breakfast, a bath and a shampoo, Lizzie felt fully recovered from her ordeal. She dressed in clothes Lorelei had purchased for her at the mercantile, a green woolen dress with lace at the collar, lovely sheer stockings and fashionable high-button shoes.

"You mustn't overdo," Lorelei fretted. Usually a practical person, today Lizzie's stepmother seemed almost fragile. The shadows under her eyes indicated that she'd worried a great deal over the past few days, and gotten little or no sleep.

"Lorelei," Lizzie said, placing her hands on her stepmother's pale cheeks, "I'm home. I'm *fine.* You said it yourself—I'm McKettrick tough."

"I was so frightened," Lorelei confessed, with an uncharacteristic sniffle.

The two women embraced, clung tightly.

"I want to look in on the others," Lizzie said, when they'd drawn apart. "Morgan—Dr. Shane—first. Then Whitley and Mr. and Mrs. Thaddings and the Halifaxes and John Brennan and Mr. Christian—"

Lorelei frowned. "Mr. Christian? I recall the other names—and I met Dr. Shane last night. But no one mentioned a Mr. Christian."

"You must have seen him," Lizzie insisted. "He was very ill—with frostbite—and he would have needed tending. I'll ask Morgan."

Lorelei still seemed puzzled. "Perhaps I'm mistaken," she said doubtfully. Lorelei McKettrick was rarely mistaken about anything, and everyone knew it. She paused, rallied a little. "I'd better round up your brothers. They must have finished breakfast by now, and my guess is, they'll be up to mischief pretty soon."

Lizzie and Lorelei went down the stairs together and parted in the lobby. Lizzie immediately noticed Whitley sitting alone in a leather chair, his injured leg propped on an ottoman, gazing out at the snowy street beyond the window. He looked almost forlorn.

Procrastinating, Lizzie decided resolutely, would only make matters worse. She approached, cleared her throat softly when Whitley didn't notice her right away.

When he did, his face lit up and he started to rise.

"Please," Lizzie said. "Don't get up."

He sank back into his chair, gestured goodnaturedly at the plaster cast replacing the improvised splint Morgan had applied onboard the stranded train. "Modern medicine," he said. "I'll be walking properly within six weeks."

"That's wonderful," Lizzie said, wringing her hands a little, then quickly tucking them behind her back. "I'm . . . I'm so sorry, Whitley."

"For what?" he asked.

"Getting you into all this," Lizzie answered, flustered. "Inviting you here—You wouldn't have broken your leg if I hadn't, or nearly perished in an avalanche—"

Whitley's smile faded, and he tried to stand again.

To keep him in his chair, Lizzie drew up a second ottoman and perched on it, facing him.

"Lizzie?" he prompted when she didn't say anything right away. She, affectionately known on the Triple M as "chatterbox," couldn't seem to find words.

"I saw the ring," she said. "When I took your good overcoat out of your trunk to put under the Christmas tree for John Brennan."

"Ah," Whitley said, still unsmiling. "The ring. It belonged to my grandmother, you know. I had it reset, before we left San Francisco."

Pain flashed through Lizzie. For a moment, she actually considered accepting Whitley's ring, going through with the wedding, just to keep from dashing his hopes. Reason soon prevailed—she'd do him far greater harm if she trapped him in a loveless marriage. "It's very beautiful," she said sadly.

Whitley's face filled with eagerness and hope. "Will you marry me, Lizzie? I know this isn't the most romantic proposal, and I don't even have the ring to put on your finger, since it's still in my trunk and none of our things have been recovered from the train yet, but I've already spoken to your father—"

"Whitley," Lizzie said, almost moaning the name, *"stop."*

"Lizzie—"

"No," she whispered raggedly. "Please. I can't marry you, Whitley. I don't . . . I don't love you."

"You'll *learn* to love me—"

Lizzie shook her head.

Whitley reddened. "It's Shane, isn't it? He's stolen you away from me, turned your head, acting like a hero on the train—"

Again Lizzie shook her head. Then she couldn't bear it any longer, and she got to her feet and turned to flee, only to collide hard with Morgan.

Chapter Seven

Morgan gripped Lizzie's shoulders gently and steadied her. Spoke her name in a worried rasp. Behind her, Lizzie heard Whitley shoving to his feet, and his anger struck her back like a flood of something hot and dark.

"What can he give you?" Whitley demanded furiously. "Tell me what *Dr.* Morgan Shane can give you that I can't!"

Mortified, Lizzie gazed helplessly up into Morgan's concerned face. She saw a muscle twitch in his strong jawline, and his gaze sliced past her to Whitley.

His expression strained—he was clearly trying to rein in his temper—Morgan pressed Lizzie into a nearby chair and turned on Whitley.

"What the *hell* is going on here?" he growled.

Awash in misery and abject humiliation, Lizzie sat up very straight and breathed deeply. She had not turned down Whitley's proposal precisely because of her feelings for Morgan, though they had certainly been part of her reasoning. Now Morgan would think she'd set her cap for him, refused Whitley so she could pursue Indian Rock's handsome new doctor instead.

In fact, she hadn't decided anything of the kind. Yes, she was drawn to Morgan, profoundly so, but it was far too soon to know if the attraction would last. And how in the *world* was she going to look him directly in the eye, after a scene like this?

"You took advantage!" Whitley shouted at Morgan, every word ricocheting off Lizzie's most tender places like a stone flung hard and true to its mark.

"Sit down, before you fall over," Morgan replied, his voice ominously calm. "And may I remind you that this is a public place?"

Lizzie couldn't look at either of them. Indeed, it was all she could do not to cover her face with both hands in absolute mortification.

"What can you give her, Shane?" Whitley persisted, sputtering now. "Tell me that! A name? A respectable home? Money?" He paused, gathering his forces to go on. "*My* family has a mansion on Nob Hill and a place in San Francisco society. Our name—"

Out of the corner of her eye, Lizzie saw her grandfather striding toward them, from the direction of the hotel dining room. "Lizzie *has* a name—a fine one," Angus boomed. "It's McKettrick. And she'll never lack for money or a 'respectable home,' either!"

Lizzie risked a glance at Morgan and saw that he looked confounded and not a little angry. He must have felt her gaze, because he returned it, though only briefly, a sharp, cutting edge.

"It is my understanding," he said coolly, ignoring Angus and Lizzie, too, "that Miss McKettrick intends to teach school, rather than marry. If she's spurned you, Carson, you have my sympathies, but her decision has nothing to do with me. And if you want your nose broken as well as your leg, just keep raving like a lunatic. I'll be happy to oblige."

At last, drawing some quiet strength from her grandfather's presence, Lizzie managed to look directly, and steadily, at Whitley and Morgan. They were standing dangerously close to each other, their hands clenched into fists at their sides, their eyes blazing.

"Reminds me of a couple of bucks facing off in rutting season," Angus observed, looking and sounding amused, now that he knew what the ruckus was about, and that his granddaughter was in no physical danger.

Lizzie blushed so hard her cheeks ached. "Whitley misunderstood," she told Morgan, after swallowing hard. "When I told him I couldn't accept his proposal, he jumped to the conclusion that . . . that something was happening between you and me."

"Imagine that," Morgan said, his tone scathing.

Inside, where no one could see, Lizzie flinched.

Outside, she wore her fierce McKettrick pride like an inflexible garment. "Imagine that indeed," she retorted, as a frown took shape on Angus's face. "It just so happens that I'm not the least bit interested in *either* of you."

With that, she made for the doorway leading onto the street.

As she left, she heard mutters from both Whitley and Morgan, and a low burst of laughter from her grandfather.

At least Lizzie wasn't going to marry Carson, Morgan reflected, while he willed himself to simmer down. His pride stung, he'd retreated to his office, and once there, he took a fresh look around.

Carson was right. Morgan couldn't offer Lizzie a mansion, or a name more prominent than the one she already had. God knew, he didn't have money, either.

Saddened, Morgan went on through the office and into his living quarters—the stove, the bulky bathtub, the too-narrow bed. He couldn't imagine Lizzie living happily in such a place—though the bed had a certain delicious potential—when she was used to big ranch houses, fancy schools, the best of everything.

He heard the office door open, shoved a hand through his hair and went to see if he had a patient. He found Angus McKettrick looming in the examining room, which must have seemed hardly larger than a tobacco tin to a man of his size and stature. White-haired and wise-eyed, McKettrick studied Morgan.

"Where there's smoke," he said, in that portentous voice of his, "there's bound to be fire."

Morgan studied him, at a loss for a response.

"Our Lizzie-bet," Angus went on, after indulging in a crooked little smile and folding arms the size of tree trunks, "is too much woman for most men."

Morgan felt his neck heat up. "Lizzie's independent-minded, all right," he agreed evenly. "But if you're here because you think I wrecked her marriage plans with Mr. Nob Hill out there, I didn't."

"Oh, I believe you did," Angus said complacently. "You just don't seem to *know* it."

Something inside Morgan soared, then dived straight back to hard ground, landing with shattering impact. "You heard Lizzie," he said, when he was fairly certain he could speak rationally. "She's not interested in Carson *or* me."

"So she says," Angus drawled. "I don't think Lizzie knows what's going on here any more than you do."

"Look around you," Morgan bit out, waving one hand for emphasis. "This is what I have to offer your granddaughter."

"Not much to it," Angus agreed, his tone dry, his eyes twinkling. "But I think there's something to *you,* Dr. Shane. You've got some gumption and grit, the way I hear it, and Lizzie's cut from the same kind of cloth. She'd climb straight up the velvet draperies, penned up in some fancy house in San Francisco. She's a country girl, and something of a tomboy. She sits a horse as well as any of us, and she can shoot, too. Before you go deciding you don't have what she needs, you might want to spend a little time finding out just what that is."

The old man's words nettled Morgan and, at the same time, gave him hope. "What makes you think I'm interested in Lizzie?" he asked.

Angus merely chuckled. Shook his head.

And, having said his piece, he turned and left Morgan's office, the door standing wide open behind him.

Lizzie stormed toward nothing in particular, delighting in the bracing chill of the winter air as she left the Arizona Hotel, the familiar sights and sounds surrounding her, the hustle and bustle of wagons, buckboards and buggies weaving through the snowy street. Furious tears scalded her cheeks, and she wiped them away with a dash of one hand, walking faster and then faster still.

When she found herself in front of the mercantile, its wide display window cheerfully festooned with bright ribbon and evergreen boughs, she stopped, drew a deep breath and went inside.

The scent of Christmas assailed her—a tall pine stood in the center of the general store, bedecked with costly German ornaments, shining and new.

Brightly wrapped gifts, probably empty, encircled the base of the tree.

A woman in her early thirties rounded the counter, smiling. She wore a practical dress of lightweight gray woolen, and her blond hair, pinned into a loose chignon at her nape, escaped in wisps around her delicate face. Her eyes were a shining blue, and they smiled at Lizzie a fraction of a moment before her bow-shaped mouth followed suit.

"Aren't they lovely?" the woman asked, apparently referring to the blown-glass balls and angels and St. Nicholases shimmering on the fragrant tree.

Lizzie nodded. She had not come into the mercantile to admire the merchandise, but to inquire after John Brennan. When she'd last seen him, he'd been desperately ill. "Mrs. Brennan?" she asked.

The woman nodded. Approached Lizzie and put out a hand. "Call me Alice," she said. "You must be Lizzie McKettrick. John told me how kind you were to him."

Lizzie swallowed. "Is he—is he better?"

Alice Brennan smiled. She was as pretty, and as fragile, as the most delicate of the tree ornaments. "He's holding on," she said, worry flickering in her eyes. "Would you like to see him?"

"I wouldn't want to disturb his rest," Lizzie said.

"I think he'd welcome a visit from you," Alice replied, turning slightly, beckoning for Lizzie to follow her.

Lizzie did follow, at once reluctant to impose on

the Brennans and eager to see John and measure his progress with her own eyes.

There were stairs at the back of the large store, behind cloth curtains. Alice led the way up, with Lizzie a few steps behind.

The family living quarters above were spare, by comparison to downstairs, where every shelf and surface was stuffed with merchandise of various kinds, but a large iron cookstove chortled out heat in one corner, and there was a smaller Christmas tree on a table in front of the windows overlooking the street.

John Brennan lay, cosseted in blankets, on a settee. He smiled wanly when he saw Alice.

"I've brought you a visitor," Alice told her husband.

A little boy, undoubtedly Tad, sat on the floor near the settee, playing with a carved wooden horse. He looked up at Lizzie with benign curiosity, then went back to galloping the toy horse across a plain of pillows.

John beamed when he saw Lizzie; he'd been lying prone when she came in, and now he tried to sit up, but he was weak, and failed in the effort. Alice bent to kiss his forehead, smooth his hair back, murmur something to him. Then she stepped back and, with a gesture of one hand, offered Lizzie a seat in a sturdy wing-back chair nearby.

Lizzie sat, feeling like an intruder.

"You said I'd get home to Alice and the boy," John said, his eyes shining, "and here I am."

Lizzie only smiled, blinked back tears. John

Brennan was home, but he was still a very sick man, obviously, and hardly out of danger. Had he survived the ordeal on the train, and the rigorous journey to Indian Rock by horse-drawn sleigh, only to succumb to pneumonia after all?

"I reckon if you say I'll get well," John labored to add, "that will happen, too. There's something real special about you, Lizzie McKettrick."

Lizzie's throat ached. "You'll get well," she said, more because she *wanted* to believe than because she did. Alas, there was no magic in her, as John seemed to think. She was an ordinary woman. "You've got little Tad to raise, and Alice and her folks will need your help running the store."

John nodded, relaxed a little, as though Lizzie had given him some vital gift by saying what he needed to hear. "You seem to be holding up all right," he said, the words rattling up out of his thin chest.

"I'll be fine," she said, and she knew that was true, at least. She'd hurt Whitley, and alienated Morgan in the process, but she still had her family, her friends, her teaching certificate, her future. John Brennan might not be that lucky.

"The others?" John asked.

She told him what she could about their fellow passengers—Whitley, the Halifaxes, Morgan. Mr. and Mrs. Thaddings, who were staying, according to Lorelei, in Clarinda Adams's house. She spoke of everyone except Mr. Christian; for some reason, she was hesitant to mention him.

"That's good," he said, and Lizzie saw that he could barely keep his eyes open. She'd stayed too long—it was past time for her to be on her way.

"Is there anything I can do to help?" she asked Alice, at the top of the stairs.

"Just pray," Alice said. "And come back to visit when you can. It heartens John, receiving company."

Lizzie nodded.

There had been no sign of Alice's parents, who actually owned the mercantile, according to what John had told her on the train. She'd meet them later, she was sure, since Indian Rock was a small town and she'd be trading at the store regularly, once she moved into the little room behind the schoolhouse.

Outside again, Lizzie decided she wasn't ready to go back to the hotel. Lorelei would insist that she lie down again, and even if she managed to avoid Morgan and Whitley as she passed through the lobby, she would still be painfully aware of their presence.

She pulled her cloak, provided by Lorelei, more tightly around her, raised the hood to protect her ears from the clear but bitter cold and proceeded along the sidewalk, again with no particular destination in mind. She wasn't headed *toward* anything, she realized uncomfortably, but *away* from Whitley's anger and Morgan's terse dismissal.

She went to the schoolhouse, a red-painted framework building with a tiny bell tower and quarters in back, for the teacher. Her aunt Chloe, Jeb's wife, had once taught here, and made her home in the little room behind the classroom.

All the doors were locked, but she stood on tiptoe to peer in a window at what would be her home directly after New Year's, when she took up her duties. There was a little stove, an iron bedstead, a table and chair and not much else. She'd looked so forward to teaching school, earning her own money, paltry though her salary was, shaping the lives of children in small but important ways.

Now it seemed a lonely prospect, as empty as those cheery packages under the Christmas tree in the mercantile.

She sighed and turned from the window and was startled to find Mr. Christian standing directly behind her. He looked particularly hearty, showing no signs of frostbite or exhaustion. In fact, there seemed to be a faint glow to his skin, and his eyes shone with well-being.

He touched the brim of his bowler hat. Smiled.

Lizzie felt something warm inside her, despite the unrelenting cold. "I'm so glad to see you," she said. "No one seems to remember—"

"No one seems to remember what?" Christian asked kindly. He wore a very fine overcoat, one Lizzie hadn't seen before, and his hands bulged in the deep pockets.

"Well," Lizzie said, groping a little, *"you."*

Mr. Christian smiled again. "Dr. Shane remembers," he said. "And the children will, too. Little Ellen and Jack will remember—always."

The oddness of the remark struck Lizzie, but she was so pleased to see that her friend had recovered that she paid little mind to it. "I've just been to visit John Brennan," she said. "I'm afraid—"

Mr. Christian cut her off with a kindly shake of his head. "He'll recover," he said with certainty.

Lizzie frowned, puzzled. "How can you be so sure?"

"Call it a Christmas miracle," Mr. Christian said.

A little thrill tripped down Lizzie's spine. The freezing air seemed charged somehow, as though electricity had gathered around the two of them, silent, a small, invisible tornado. "I'd like to introduce you to my stepmother, Lorelei," she said, after a moment in which her heart seemed to snag on something sharp.

"Because she doesn't believe I exist?" Mr. Christian asked, his smile muted now, and full of quiet amusement.

Lizzie sighed. "Not *only* that," she protested. "Lorelei probably knows your family and—"

"I have no family, Lizzie. Not the kind you mean, anyway."

"But you said—"

Again, the faint and mysterious smile came. The glow Lizzie had noticed before intensified a little. And it came to her that Mr. Christian simply could not have recovered so completely in such a short time. Had he . . . died? Was she seeing his ghost? She'd heard of things like that, of course, but never given them serious consideration before that moment.

"Who are you?" she heard herself ask, in a near whisper.

He didn't answer.

Lizzie reached out, meaning to clutch at his sleeve, a way of insisting that he reply, but grab though she might, she couldn't seem to catch hold of him. It was the strangest sensation—he was *there,* not transparent as she imagined a spirit might be, but a real person, one of reality and substance. Without moving at all, he still managed to evade her touch.

"Who are you?" she repeated, more forcefully this time.

"That's not important," he said quietly. Then he pointed to someone or something just past Lizzie's left shoulder. "Look there," he added. "There's your young man, coming to make things up. Give him every opportunity, Lizzie. He's the one."

Lizzie turned to look, saw Morgan vaulting over the schoolyard fence, starting toward her. She turned again, with another question for Mr. Christian teetering on the tip of her tongue, but he was gone.

Simply *gone.*

Startled, her heart pounding, Lizzie swept the large yard, but there was no sign of Mr. Christian. She hurried to look behind the building, but he wasn't there, either. Nor was he behind the outhouse or the little shed meant to house a horse or a milk cow.

"Lizzie?"

She whirled.

Morgan stood at her side. "What's the matter?" he asked, frowning.

"Mr. Christian," she sputtered. "He was just here—surely you must have seen him—"

Morgan frowned. "I didn't see anybody but you," he said, taking her arm. "Are you all right?"

She was shaking. She felt like laughing—and like crying. Like dancing, and like collapsing in a heap in the powdery snow.

The snow.

She searched the ground—Mr. Christian would have left footprints in the snow, just as she had. But there were no tracks, other than her own and Morgan's.

She sagged against Morgan, stunned, and his arms tightened around her. "Lizzie!" There was a plea in his voice. *Be all right,* it said.

"I . . . I must be seeing things—" She gulped in a breath, shook her head. "No. I *did* see Mr. Christmas—*Mr. Christian*—he was right here. We spoke . . . he told me—"

"Lizzie," Morgan repeated, gripping her upper arms now, looking deep into her eyes. "Stop chattering and *breathe.*"

"He was here!"

Morgan led her around to the front of the schoolhouse, sat her down on the side of the porch, where the snow had melted away, took a seat beside her. "I believe you," he said, holding her hand. She felt his innate strength, strength of mind and spirit and body, flowing into her, buoying her up. Sustaining her. "Lizzie, *I believe you.*"

She let her head rest against his shoulder, not caring who saw her and Morgan, sitting close together on the schoolhouse porch, holding hands, even though it was highly improper.

For a long while, neither of them spoke. Lizzie was willing her heartbeat to return to normal, and Morgan seemed content just to be there with her.

Finally, though, he broke the silence. "You're really not going to marry Carson?" he asked, looking as sheepish as he sounded.

"I'm really not going to marry Whitley," Lizzie confirmed. Her heart started beating fast again.

"He was right," Morgan went on, after heaving a resigned sigh. He gazed off toward the distant mountain, where they'd been stranded together, nearly buried under tons of snow. "About all the things he said earlier, back at the hotel, I mean. I can't offer you what he can. No position in society. No mansion. No money to speak of."

Lizzie blinked, studied him. "Morgan Shane," she said, "*look* at me."

He obeyed, grinned sadly.

"What are you saying?" she asked.

He hesitated for what seemed to Lizzie an excruciatingly long time. Then, with another sigh, he answered her question with one of his own. "Can you imagine yourself being courted by a penniless country doctor with no prospects to speak of?"

Lizzie's breath caught. She considered the matter for all of two seconds. "Yes," she said. "I can imagine that very well."

He enclosed the hand he'd been holding in both his own, looked straight into Lizzie's soul. "I know it will take time. There's a lot we don't know about each other. You've got classes to teach, and I'll be building a medical practice. But if you'll have me, Lizzie McKettrick, I'll be your husband by this time next year."

"D-do you love me?" Lizzie asked, color flaring in her cheeks at the audacity of her question.

"I'm pretty sure I do," Morgan replied, with a saucy grin. "Do you love me?"

"I certainly feel *something,*" Lizzie said, blissfully bewildered. "But I'm not sure I trust myself. After all, I thought I loved Whitley. All I could think about, before we left San Francisco—" *before I met you* "—was whether he'd propose to me over Christmas or not."

Morgan chuckled.

"I guess it proves something my grandfather always says," Lizzie went on. "Be careful what you wish for, because you might damn well get it."

This time Morgan laughed out loud. "Amen," he said.

Lizzie turned thoughtful. "I'd want to go right on teaching school, even if we got married," she warned.

"And I'll want children," Morgan said.

A great joy swelled inside Lizzie, one she could barely contain. "At least four," she agreed. "Two girls and two boys."

Morgan's eyes gleamed. "The room behind my office might get a little crowded," he told her.

"We'll think of something," Lizzie said.

"The hardest part will be waiting," Morgan told her, leaning in a little, lowering his voice. "To get those babies started, I mean."

Lizzie blushed, well aware of his meaning. She'd never been intimate with a man, not even Whitley, though she'd allowed him to kiss her a few times, but she craved *this* man, this "penniless country doctor," with her entire being. She wondered if she could endure a whole year of such wanting.

Reading her expression, Morgan chuckled again, rested his forehead against hers. "I'm about to kiss you, Lizzie McKettrick," he said. "Like I've wanted to kiss you from the moment I first laid eyes on you. And if the whole town of Indian Rock sees me do that, so be it."

Lizzie swallowed, tilted her head upward, ready for his kiss. Longing for it. And feeling utterly scandalized by the ferocity of her own desire.

He laid his mouth to hers, gently at first, then with a hunger to match and even exceed her own. His lips felt deliciously warm, despite the frigid weather, and wonderfully soft. She trembled as the kiss deepened, caught fire inside when his tongue found hers. It was a foretaste of things to come, things that could only happen when they were married, but she felt it in her most feminine parts, as surely as if he'd laid her down on that schoolhouse porch and taken her outright, made her his own.

She moaned.

Morgan's soft laugh echoed in her mouth.

He knew. He *knew* what she was thinking, what she was feeling.

Lizzie's face felt as hot as the blood singing through her veins.

"Oh, my goodness," she gasped, when the kiss was over.

"Only the beginning," Morgan promised gruffly, twisting a loose tendril of her hair gently around one finger.

"Hush," she said helplessly.

He let go of her face, which he'd been holding between his hands while he kissed her, while he *possessed* her, and put a slight but eloquent distance between them. "I'd better get back to the hotel," he said. "I'm expecting some patients, now that I've figuratively hung out my shingle."

"I'll go with you," Lizzie said, not because she particularly wanted to return to the hotel, where she would be treated like an invalid, albeit a cherished one, but because she couldn't be parted from Morgan.

Not yet. Not after what had just happened between them—whatever it was.

As Lizzie had expected, word had gotten around that the new doctor was young, handsome and eligible. Three women, all of them known to Lizzie and notoriously single, awaited him, in varying stages of feigned illness.

She had the silliest urge to shoo them away, like so many hens fluttering around a rooster. Fortunately, she recovered her good sense in time, and simply smiled.

Whitley had left the lobby, perhaps retreating to his nearby room, and Lizzie was relieved by that. She'd be glad when he left Indian Rock, but she knew it might be a while before the train ran again, and the roads were all but impassable.

Suddenly hungry, she made her way through the empty dining room to the kitchen, and found Lorelei there, chatting with the Chinese cook.

"There you are," Lorelei said, in a tone of good-natured scolding. "Your cheeks are flushed. Have you taken a chill?"

Lizzie still felt the tingle of Morgan's kiss on her mouth, and things had melted inside her, so that she was a little unsteady on her feet. She sank into a rocking chair near the stove, smiling foolishly. "No," she said. "I haven't taken a chill. But I'm famished."

The cook dished up a bowl of beef stew dolloped with dumplings and handed it to Lizzie where she sat, along with a spoon, then left.

Lorelei drew up a second chair.

"Something very strange happened to me today," Lizzie confided, without really intending to, between bites of savory stew.

"I saw you come in with Dr. Shane," Lorelei said, with a gentle but knowing smile. "Lizzie McKettrick, I do believe you've fallen in love."

Perhaps she *had* fallen in love, Lizzie thought. Time would tell.

"Lizzie?" Lorelei prompted, when Lizzie didn't confirm or deny her stepmother's assertion.

"He's going to court me," she said. "Do you think Papa will object?"

"No," Lorelei responded, watching Lizzie very closely. "Would it matter if he did?"

Lizzie laughed. "No," she said. "I don't think it would."

Lorelei smiled, her eyes glistening with happy tears. "It's love, all right. When I met your father, I figured we were all wrong for each other, and I wanted to be with him so badly that I couldn't think straight."

"Something else happened," Lizzie went on, because there was very little she didn't share with her stepmother. Quietly, carefully, she told Lorelei about her encounter with Mr. Christian, at the schoolyard, leaving nothing out.

"Good heavens," Lorelei said, when the tale was told. Then she reached out and tested Lizzie's fore-head for fever. Finding her flesh cool, she frowned and managed to look relieved at one and the same time.

"You believe me, don't you?" Lizzie asked shyly.

"If you say you saw this Mr. Christian," Lorelei said, without hesitation, "then you saw him. You are no flibbertigibbet, Lizzie McKettrick."

"But how could he have just—just *disappeared* that way?"

"I don't have the faintest idea," Lorelei answered. Then she rose from her chair. "Finish your stew. I'll be back in a few minutes, and we'll have tea."

Lizzie nodded and her stepmother hurried out of the kitchen, only to be replaced by Angus. He helped himself to a cup of coffee from the pot on the stove and stood watching Lizzie curiously, as though she'd changed in some fundamental way.

And perhaps she had.

"You did a fine job after that avalanche," he told her. "Looking after folks. Trying to keep their spirits up."

"Thank you," Lizzie said. Hers was an independent spirit, but she valued her grandfather's opinion of her, along with those of Lorelei and, of course, her papa.

He sipped his coffee. "You're all right, aren't you, Lizzie-girl? You seem—well—different."

"It's possible I'm in love," she said.

Angus smiled, lifted his coffee cup as if in a toast. "I'll drink to that," he replied, just as Lorelei returned to the kitchen, carrying a Bible.

Lizzie set aside her bowl of stew, and Lorelei practically shoved the Good Book under her nose.

"Read this," she ordered, pointing to a passage in Hebrews, thirteenth chapter, second verse:

"Be not forgetful to entertain strangers; for thereby some have entertained angels unawares."

Chapter Eight

"Mr. Christian makes an unlikely angel," Lizzie told Morgan, standing in his examining room, several hours after Lorelei had shown her the Bible verse in the hotel kitchen. "Don't you think?"

Morgan pulled his stethoscope from around his neck and set it aside. "Not having made the acquaintance of all that many angels," he replied, "I couldn't say."

"He played cards with the children," Lizzie said, groping for reasons why Mr. Christian could not be a part of the heavenly host. "He pulled a gun on Whitley once, and he gave you *whiskey* when you went out into the blizzard—"

"Positively demonic," Morgan teased. "I guess I missed the part where he drew a gun."

"You were outside," Lizzie answered.

"Why would a peddler feel compelled to threaten Carson with a gun, annoying though he is?"

Lizzie shook off the question. "I'm *trying* to make some sense of what happened, Morgan," Lizzie protested, "and you are not helping."

He grinned. "Some things just don't make sense, Lizzie McKettrick," he said. "Like why every unmarried woman in Indian Rock seems to have developed some fetching and very melodramatic malady."

Lizzie laughed, though she wasn't amused. "No mystery to that," she answered. "You're an eligible bachelor, after all."

He moved closer to her, rested his hands on her shoulders. "Oh, but I'm *not* eligible," he said, his low voice setting things aquiver inside Lizzie. "I'm definitely taken."

He was about to kiss her again, but the office door crashed open with a terrible bang, and both of them turned to see Doss, Lizzie's seven-year-old brother, standing on the threshold.

"Pa's back!" he shouted exuberantly. "The roads are clear, and after church, we can go home and have Christmas!" He paused, his small face screwed into a puzzled frown. "Were you *smooching?*" he demanded, looking suspicious.

Lizzie laughed, and so did Morgan.

"No," Lizzie said.

"Yes," Morgan replied, at the same moment.

"You'd better get married, then," Doss decided. "You're not supposed to kiss people if you're not married to them."

"Is that right?" Morgan asked, approaching Doss and ruffling his thick blond hair.

"I bet it says so in the Bible," Doss insisted solemnly.

"Do we have a budding preacher in our midst?" Morgan asked Lizzie, his eyes full of warm laughter.

Lizzie giggled. "Doss? Perish the thought. He's more imp than angel."

At the word *angel,* a little silence fell. Lizzie thought of Mr. Christian, of course, and the insoluble mystery he represented.

"We had to wait to have Christmas," Doss complained. "There are a whole *bunch* of packages under our tree at home, and some of them are mine. And now we have to sit through *church,* too."

Lizzie's attention was on Morgan. "Will you come with us?" she asked. "To celebrate a McKettrick Christmas, I mean?"

Morgan looked reluctant. "I'd be intruding," he said.

"That man with the broken leg is going," Doss put in, relentlessly helpful.

Morgan merely spread his hands to Lizzie, as if to say *I told you so.*

"You belong with us," Lizzie said, not to be put off. It would be awkward, celebrating their delayed Christmas with both Whitley and Morgan present, but that was unavoidable. To leave Whitley alone at the hotel while everyone else enjoyed roast goose and eggnog was simply not the McKettrick way.

In the end Morgan relented.

Pastor Reynolds held a Christmas Eve service at sunset, and the whole town attended. Candles were lit, carols were sung, a gentle sermon was preached. After the closing prayer, gifts were given out to all the children, and Lizzie recognized her father's handiwork, made in his woodshop, and the cloth dolls and animals Lorelei and the aunts had sewn. Every child received a present.

Mr. and Mrs. Thaddings watched fondly, and somewhat wistfully, Lizzie thought, as Ellen Halifax showed off the doll she'd wanted so much. Jack received a stick horse with a yarn mane, and galloped up and down the aisle, despite his mother's protests. John and Alice Brennan were there, too, with Alice's parents and little Tad, who seemed fascinated with his toy buckboard.

Lizzie approached the Thaddingses. She knew Pastor Reynolds had wired Clarinda Adams on their behalf, hoping she'd allow them to stay on until she either returned or sold the house, but there hadn't been time for an answer.

Mrs. Thaddings embraced her. "You look well, Lizzie," she said.

"I'm happy to be home," Lizzie replied. Whitley, standing nearby, letting his crutches support his weight, looked despondent. She wondered if he'd ever considered staying on in Indian Rock, or if he'd always intended to insist they live in San Francisco, after they were married.

She would probably never know, she decided. And it didn't matter.

"We'd better get back and see to Woodrow, dear,"

Mr. Thaddings told his wife, taking a gentle hold on her elbow. "Before this snow gets too deep."

Lizzie wasn't about to let the Thaddingses walk home, and quickly conscripted her goodnatured uncle Jeb to drive them in his buggy.

Later, when the McKettrick clan left Indian Rock for the Triple M, Morgan was with them, seated next to Lizzie in the back of her father's wagon. Whitley, alternately scowling and looking bleak, rode in the other. The snow, so threatening on the mountain, fell like a blessed benediction all around them, soothing and soft, almost magical.

The first sight of the main ranch house brought tears to Lizzie's eyes. She'd thought, before the rescue, that she might never see the home place again, never warm herself before one of the fires, dream in a rocking chair while a summer rain pattered at the roof. But there it was, sturdy and dearly familiar, its roof laced with snow, its windows alight with a golden glow.

Dogs barked a merry greeting, and small cousins, as well as aunts and uncles, poured from wagons and buckboards, their voices a happy buzz in the wintry darkness.

Lizzie stood still, after Morgan helped her down from the wagon, taking it all in. Hiding things in her heart.

Inside her grandfather's house, a giant tree winked with tinsel. Piles of packages stood beneath it, some simply wrapped in brown paper or newsprint, others bedecked in pretty cloth and tied with shimmering ribbons.

Concepcion, her grandfather's wife, must have been cooking for days. The house was redolent with the aromas Lizzie had yearned for on the stranded train—freshly baked bread, savory roast goose, spices like cinnamon and nutmeg. Lizzie breathed deeply of the love and happiness surrounding her on all sides.

The children were excited, of course, all the more so because, for them, Christmas was just plain late. At Holt's suggestion, they were allowed to empty their bulging St. Nicholas stockings and open their packages.

Chaos reigned while dolls and games and brightly colored shirts and dresses were unwrapped. Lizzie watched the whole scene in a daze of gratitude and love for her large, boisterous family. Morgan stood nearby, enjoying the melee, while Whitley slumped in a leather chair next to the fireplace, wearing an expression that said, "Bah, humbug."

If she hadn't known it before, Lizzie would have known then that Whitley simply didn't belong with this rowdy crew. Morgan, on the other hand, had soon taken off his coat, pushed up his sleeves and knelt on the floor to help Doss assemble a miniature ranch house from a toy set of interlocking logs.

A nudge from her father distracted Lizzie, and she started when she saw what he was holding in his hands—Mr. Christian's music box, the one he'd given her on Christmas Eve, aboard the train.

She blinked. Surely they'd left it behind, along with most of their other possessions, to be collected later.

"The tag says it's for you," Holt said, looking puzzled. Clearly, he didn't recall seeing the music box before.

Lizzie's hands trembled as she accepted the box. A strain of "O Little Town of Bethlehem" tinkled from its depths, so ethereal that she was sure, in the moment after, that she'd imagined it.

She found a chair—not easy since the house was bulging with McKettricks—and sank into it, stricken speechless.

Whitley, as it happened, already occupied the chair next to hers. He frowned, eyeing the music box resting in Lizzie's lap like some sacred object to be guarded at all costs.

"That's pretty," he said, with a grudging note to his voice. "Did Shane give it to you?"

Lizzie shook her head, made herself meet Whitley's gaze. "Don't you remember, Whitley?" she asked, referring to Christmas Eve on the train, when they'd *all* seen the music box, listened with sad delight to its chiming tunes.

"Remember what?" Whitley asked. He wasn't pretending, Lizzie knew. He honestly didn't recall either the music box *or* Mr. Christian.

"Never mind," Lizzie said.

Dinner was announced, and Whitley got up, reaching for his crutches, and stumped off toward the dining room. Most of the children had fallen asleep on piles of crumpled wrapping paper, and the adults had all gone to eat.

All except Morgan, and Lizzie herself, that is.

"Hungry?" Morgan asked, extending a hand to Lizzie.

She set the music box aside, on the sturdy table next to her chair, and took Morgan's hand. "Starved," she said.

Instead of escorting her into the dining room, where everyone else had gathered—their voices were like a muted symphony of laughter and happy conversation, sweet to Lizzie's ears—Morgan drew her close. Held her as though they were about to swirl into the flow of a waltz.

"If what I'm feeling right now isn't love," Morgan said, his lips nearly touching Lizzie's, "then there's something even *better* than love."

Lizzie's throat constricted. She whispered his name, and he would have kissed her, she supposed, if a third party hadn't made his presence known with a clearing of the throat.

"Time for that later," Angus said, grinning. "Supper's on the table."

By New Year's, the tracks had been cleared and the trains were running again. Lizzie waited on the platform, alongside Whitley, the sole traveler leaving Indian Rock that day.

A cold, dry wind blew, stinging Lizzie's ears, and she felt as miserable as Whitley looked.

You'll meet someone else.

That was what she wanted to say, but it seemed presumptuous, under the circumstances. Whitley's feelings were private ones, and she had no real way of knowing what they were.

"You're sure about this?" he asked quietly, as the train rounded the bend in the near distance, whistle blowing, white steam chuffing from the smokestack against a brittle blue sky. "We could have a good life together, Lizzie."

Lizzie blinked back tears. Yes, she supposed they *could* have a good life together, she and Whitley, good enough, anyway. But she wanted more than "good enough," for herself and Morgan—and for Whitley. "You belong in San Francisco," she told him gently. "And I belong right here, in Indian Rock."

Whitley surprised her with a sad, tender smile. "I hate to admit it," he said, "but you're probably right. Be happy, Lizzie."

The train was nearly at the platform now, and so loud that Lizzie would have had to shout to be heard over the din. So she stood on tiptoe and planted a brief, chaste kiss on Whitley's mouth.

Metal brakes squealed as the train came to a full stop.

Whitley stared into Lizzie's eyes for a long moment, saying a silent fare-thee-well, then he turned, deft on his crutches, to leave. She watched until he'd boarded the train, then turned and walked slowly away.

In the morning, her first day of teaching would commence. She headed for the schoolhouse, where her father and her uncle Jeb were unloading some of her things from the back of a buckboard.

Jeb nodded to her and smiled before lugging her rocking chair inside, but Holt came to Lizzie and slipped an arm around her shoulders. Kissed her lightly on the forehead.

"Goodbyes can be hard," he said, knowing she'd just come from the train depot, "even when it's for the best."

Lizzie nodded, choked up. "I was so sure—"

Holt chuckled. "Of course you were sure," he said. "You're a McKettrick, and McKettricks are sure of everything."

"What if I'm wrong about Morgan?" she asked, looking up into her father's face. "I don't think I could stand to say goodbye to him."

"Don't borrow trouble, Lizzie-bet," Holt smiled. "You've got a year of courting ahead of you. And my guess is, at the end of that time, you'll know for sure, one way or the other."

She nodded, swallowed, and rested her forehead against Holt's shoulder.

Later, when she'd explored her classroom, with its blackboard and potbellied stove and long, low-slung tables, for what must have been the hundredth time, she went into her living quarters.

Her father and uncle had gone, and her personal belongings were all around, in boxes and crates and travel trunks. Her books, her most serviceable dresses, a pretty china lamp from her bedroom at the ranch, the little writing desk her grandfather had given her as a Christmas gift.

Lorelei had packed quilts and sheets and fluffy pillows, meant to make the stark little room more homelike, and before they'd gone, her father and uncle had built a nice fire in the stove.

Lizzie searched until she found the music box, set it in the middle of the table, and sat down to admire it. And to wonder.

Truly, as the bard had so famously said, there *were* more things in heaven and earth than this world dreams of.

A light knock at her door brought Lizzie out of her musings, and she went to open it, found Morgan standing on the small porch facing the side yard. His hands stuffed into the pockets of his worn coat, he favored her with a shy smile.

"I know it isn't proper, but—"

"Come in," Lizzie said, catching him by the sleeve and literally pulling him over the threshold.

Inside, Morgan made such a comical effort not to notice the bed, which dominated the tiny room, that Lizzie laughed.

"I can't stay," Morgan said, making no move to leave.

"People will talk," Lizzie agreed, still amused.

His gaze strayed past her, to the music box. "This was quite a Christmas, wasn't it?" he asked.

"Quite a Christmas indeed," Lizzie said, watching as he approached the table, sorted through the stack of little brass disks containing various tunes, and slid one into the side of the music box. He wound the key, and the strains of a waltz tinkled in the air, delicate as tiny icicles dropping from the eaves of a house.

Morgan turned to Lizzie, holding out his arms, and she moved into his embrace, and they danced.

They danced until the music stopped, and then they went on dancing, in the tremulous silence that followed, around the table, past the rocking chair and the bed. Around and around and around they went, the doctor and the schoolmarm, waltzing to the beat of each other's hearts.

Chapter Nine

December 20, 1897

"Miss McKettrick?" lisped a small voice.

Lizzie looked up from the papers she'd been grading at her desk and smiled to see Tad Brennan standing there. Barely five, he was still too young to attend school, but he often showed up when classes were over for the day, to show Lizzie his "homework."

"Tad," she greeted him, cheered by his exuberant desire to learn. In the year Lizzie had been teaching, he'd mastered his alphabet and elementary arithmetic, with a lot of help from his father. By the time he officially enrolled in the fall, he'd probably be ready to skip the first grade.

"Mama says you're getting married to Dr. Shane soon," Tad said miserably.

"Well, yes," Lizzie said, resisting an urge to ruffle his hair. She knew her little brothers hated that gesture. "Dr. Shane and I *are* getting married, the day before Christmas. You're invited to the ceremony, and so are your parents and grandparents."

Tad's eyes were suddenly brilliant with tears. "That means we'll have a new teacher," he said. "And I wanted *you*."

Lizzie pushed her chair back from her desk and held out her arms to Tad. Reluctantly he allowed her to take him onto her lap. Like her brothers, he regarded himself as a big boy now, and lap sitting was suspect. "I'll be your teacher, Tad," she said gently. "The only difference will be, you'll call me Mrs. Shane instead of Miss McKettrick."

The child looked at her with mingled confusion and hope. "But aren't you going to have babies?"

Lizzie felt her cheeks warm a little. She and Morgan had done their best to wait, but one balmy night last June, the waiting had proved to be too much for both of them. They'd made love, in the deep grass of a pasture on the Triple M, and since then, they'd been together every chance they got.

"I'm sure I'll have babies," she said. "Eventually."

"Mama says women with babies have to stay home and take care of them," Tad told her solemnly.

"Does she?" Lizzie asked gently.

Tad nodded.

"Tell you what," Lizzie said, after giving him a little hug. "I promise, baby or no baby, to be here when you start first grade. Fair enough?"

Tad beamed. Nodded. Scrambled down off Lizzie's lap just as the door of the schoolhouse sprang open.

The scent of fresh evergreen filled the small room, and then Morgan was there, in the chasm, lugging a tree so large that Lizzie could only see his boots. The school's Christmas party was scheduled for the next afternoon; Lizzie and her students, fourteen children of widely varying ages, would spend the morning decorating with paper chains and bits of shiny paper garnered for the purpose.

"Miss McKettrick promised to be my teacher in first grade," Tad told Morgan seriously, "*even* if she's got a baby."

Morgan's dark eyes glinted with humor and no little passion. Late the night before, he'd knocked on Lizzie's door, and she'd let him in. He'd stayed until just before dawn, leaving Lizzie melting in the schoolteacher's bed.

"I just saw your pa," he told the child, letting the baby remark pass. "He's wanting you to help him carry in wood."

Tad said a hasty goodbye to Lizzie and hurried out. John Brennan had come a long way in the year since they'd all been stranded together in a train on the mountainside, but his health was still somewhat fragile and he counted on his son to assist him with the chores.

"Did you really meet up with John?" Lizzie asked, suspicious.

Morgan grinned, leaned the tree against the far wall and crossed the room to bend over her chair and kiss her soundly. Electricity raced along her veins and danced in her nerve endings. "I could have," he said. "Walked right past the mercantile on my way here."

Lizzie laughed, though the kiss had set her afire, as Morgan Shane's kisses always did. "You're a shameless scoundrel," she said, giving his chest a little push with both palms precisely because she wanted to pull him close instead.

"We're invited to supper at the Thaddingses'," Morgan replied, still grinning. He could turn her from a schoolmarm to a hussy within five minutes if he wanted to, and he was making sure she understood that. "They have news."

Lizzie stood up, once Morgan gave her room to do so, and began neatening the things on her desk. "News? What kind of news?"

Morgan stood behind her, pulled her back against him. She felt his desire and wondered if he'd step inside with her, after walking her back from supper at the Thaddingses', and seduce her in the little room in back. "I don't know," he murmured, his breath warm against her temple. "I guess that's why it will come as—well—*news.*"

His hands cupped her breasts, warm and strong and infinitely gentle.

"Dr. Morgan Shane," Lizzie sputtered, "this is a *schoolroom.*"

He chuckled. "So it is. I'd take you to bed and have you thoroughly, Miss McKettrick, but I saw your father and one of your uncles coming out of the Cattleman's Bank a little while ago, and my guess is, they're on their way here right now."

With a little cry, Lizzie jumped away from Morgan. Smoothed her hair and her skirts.

Sure enough, a wagon rolled clamorously up outside in the very next moment. She heard her father call out a greeting to someone passing by.

Lizzie put her hands to her cheeks, hoping to cool them. One look at her, in her present state of arousal, and her father would know what she'd been up to with Morgan. If he hadn't guessed already.

Morgan perched on the edge of her desk, folded his arms and grinned at her discomfort. "Damn," he said, "you're almost as beautiful when you want to make love as just afterward, when you make those little sighing sounds."

"Morgan!"

He laughed.

The schoolhouse door opened, and Holt McKettrick came in, dressed for winter in woolen trousers, a heavy shirt and a long coat lined in sheep's wool. His gaze moving from Morgan to Lizzie, he grinned a little.

"Lorelei sent some things in for the new house," he said. "Rafe and I will unload them over there, unless you'd rather keep them here until after the wedding."

"There would be better," Lizzie said.

Over Morgan's protests, when their engagement had become official on Lizzie's twentieth birthday in early August, her grandfather had purchased a little plot of land at the edge of town, and now a small white cottage with green-shuttered windows awaited their occupancy. Angus, Holt, the uncles and Morgan had built the place with their own hands and, little by little, it had been furnished, with one notable exception: a bed.

When Lizzie had commented on the oversight the week before, while they sat in the ranch house kitchen sewing dolls to be given away at church on Christmas Eve, her stepmother had smiled and said only, "I was your age once."

Morgan, whistling merrily under his breath, gave the evergreen a little shake, causing its scent to perfume the schoolhouse, and nodded a greeting to Holt.

"We'll be going, then," Holt said, with a note of bemused humor in his voice. His McKettrick-blue eyes twinkled. "Lorelei and the other womenfolk are wanting to fuss with your wedding dress a little more, so you'd best pay a visit to the ranch in the next day or two."

Lizzie nodded. "I'll be there," she promised.

Her papa kissed her cheek, glanced Morgan's way again and left.

As soon as Holt had gone, Morgan kissed Lizzie, too, though in an entirely different way, asked her to meet him at Clarinda Adams's place at six, and took his leave as well.

"Company!" Woodrow squawked, from inside the once-notorious Clarinda Adams house. "Company!"

Morgan smiled down at Lizzie, who stood with her cloak pulled close around her, shivering a little. The ground was blanketed with pristine white snow, and it glittered in the glow from the gas-powered streetlight on the corner. Curlicues of frost adorned the front windows. "That bird takes himself pretty seriously," Morgan observed.

"Hurry up!" Woodrow crowed. "Hurry up! No time like the present! Hurry up!"

Lizzie chuckled. The Thaddingses had become dear friends to her and to Morgan—and so had Woodrow. Once, Mr. Thaddings had even brought the bird to the schoolhouse, and the children had been fascinated by his ability to repeat everything they said to him.

The door opened, and Zebulon stood on the threshold. He wore a red silk smoking jacket, probably left behind by one of Clarinda's clients, and held a pipe in one hand. "Come in," he said. "Come in."

"Come in!" Woodrow echoed.

Gratefully, Lizzie preceded Morgan into the warm

house. Once, according to local legend, there had been paintings of naked people on the walls, but they were long gone.

Woodrow hopped on his perch. "Lizzie's here!" he cried jubilantly. "Lizzie's here!"

She laughed and, as Morgan closed the front door behind them, Woodrow flew across the entry way to land on Lizzie's shoulder.

"Lizzie's pretty," the bird went on. "Lizzie's pretty!"

"Smart bird," Morgan said, amused.

Woodrow tugged at one of the tiny combs holding Lizzie's abundance of hair in a schoolmarmish do.

"Flatterer," Zebulon scolded Woodrow affectionately. Then, to Lizzie and Morgan, he confided, "He's been after that comb all along."

Lizzie laughed again. Stroked Woodrow's top feathers with a light finger. "When are you coming back to school?" she asked him.

"Woodrow to school!" he crowed. "See the pretty birdie!"

"He'll keep this up for hours if we let him," Zebulon said, turning to lead the way into the main parlor.

Just as they reached that resplendent room, Mrs. Thaddings—Marietta, to Lizzie—entered from the dining room, carrying a tray in both hands. She was gray and frail, but Lizzie had long since stopped thinking of Marietta Thaddings as elderly. She was an active member of Indian Rock society, such as it was, hosting card clubs and giving recitations from her vast store of memorized poetry. She was the soul of kindness, and Lizzie loved her like a grandmother.

"Come, sit down by the fire," Marietta said. "I've brewed a nice pot of tea, and supper is almost ready."

Lizzie sat.

Morgan took the tray from Marietta's hands and placed it on the low table between the settee and several chairs drawn up close to the fire. Although Morgan was always polite, his solicitude worried Lizzie a little. He was, after all, Marietta's doctor as well as her friend. Was her health failing?

Marietta's eager smile belied the idea. She sat, and Woodrow flew to perch in the back of her chair.

"We've heard from Clarinda," she announced.

Lizzie braced herself. Was the legendary Miss Adams about to return to Indian Rock, and upset the proverbial apple cart? During her absence, the Thaddingses had served as caretakers of sorts. If Clarinda returned, she would almost certainly reestablish her business.

Morgan's hand landed lightly on Lizzie's shoulder, steadying her. There was so little she could hide from him; he sensed every change of mood.

"Lizzie's been a little nervous lately," he said. "What with the wedding coming up in a few days and all."

Zebulon and Marietta beamed. "So it is," Zebulon said. "Christmas Eve, after the church service the two of you will be married."

"It's so romantic," Marietta sighed sweetly.

"Let's tell them our news," Zebulon said, after giving his wife a long, adoring look.

"Clarinda has decided not to come back to Indian Rock," Marietta told them. "She hired us as permanent caretakers, and we can do what we want with the place. Turn it into a hospital or a boarding house." She paused, and she and Zebulon exchanged a glance. "Or a sort of school."

Lizzie's eyes stung with happy tears.

"We'll need to do something," Zebulon hurried to contribute. "To make ends meet, I mean, and the Territory is willing to pay us a stipend if we'll take in Indian children. The ones with no place else to go."

"You wouldn't feel we were—infringing or anything, would you, Lizzie?" Marietta asked, gently anxious.

"Infringing?" Lizzie repeated, confused. "I think it's wonderful."

Both Zebulon and Marietta sighed with relief.

"Are you up to it?" Morgan asked them, ever the practical one. "Kids are a lot of work."

Zebulon's eyes shone. "We never had children of our own, as you know, and we love them so. We'll be fine." He turned to Lizzie, looking worried again. "It will mean more pupils for you," he said. "The schoolhouse will probably have to be expanded. Usually, these little ones have been shuffled from place to place, and they're the ones without a family to take them in. They might get up to some mischief."

"After the wedding," Morgan said diplomatically, "Lizzie won't need the teacher's quarters anymore. If the town council agrees, it would be easy enough to knock out a wall and add a few desks."

Both Zebulon and Marietta looked relieved.

When it came time to serve supper, Lizzie followed Marietta back to the kitchen to help in whatever way she could.

"What's it like to live here?" she asked, because curiosity was her besetting sin and she hadn't stopped herself in time.

Marietta looked gently scandalized. "Early on, several confused gentlemen came to the door," she admitted, cheeks pink. "For a while, there, we got at least one caller every time the train stopped at the depot."

"I shouldn't have asked," Lizzie said.

"It's natural to wonder," Marietta assured her. "And Lord knows, I've done *my* share of wondering. Clarinda and I were raised in a decent, God-fearing home. My sister was always spirited, that's true, but I certainly never *dreamed* she'd grow up to run a . . . a *brothel.*"

Marietta took a roast from the oven and placed it carefully on a platter. Lizzie picked up a bowl brimming with fluffy mashed potatoes, answering, "People are full of surprises."

"Whatever she's done in the past, it's kind of

Clarinda to let Zebulon and me live here. Heaven only knows what we'd have done if she hadn't given us shelter. Why, she even wired the people at the mercantile, instructing them to let us buy whatever we needed on her account."

When the four of them were seated in the massive dining room, huddled together at one end, Zebulon offered grace. After the amen, they all ate in earnest. Woodrow remained in the parlor, squawking away.

"It hardly seems possible," Zebulon said, "that a whole year has gone by since we all met."

Morgan gave Lizzie a sidelong glance. "It seems like a long time to some of us," he said.

Lizzie elbowed him and smiled at Zebulon. "When will the children arrive?"

It was Marietta who answered. "Right after New Year's," she said. "We'll have a lot to do, Zebulon and I, to get ready."

"I can promise a whole crowd of McKettrick women to help out," Lizzie told her, with absolute confidence that it was so.

After supper, Lizzie and Marietta attended to the dishes while Zebulon, Morgan and Woodrow talked politics in the parlor.

A fresh snowfall had begun when Lizzie and Morgan left the Thaddingses' house. Instead of heading for the schoolhouse, Morgan steered Lizzie toward their cottage on the outskirts of town.

To Lizzie's surprise, lights glowed in the windows, and the tiny front room was warm when they stepped inside. They visited the house often, separately and together—Lizzie liked to imagine what it would be like, living there with Morgan, and she suspected the reverse was true, too.

The plank floors gleamed with varnish, the scent of it still sharp in the air. Two wing-backed chairs faced the small brick fireplace, and lace curtains, sewn by her stepmother and aunts, graced the many-paned windows. A hooked rug, Concepcion's handiwork, added a splash of cheery color to the room.

Dreaming, Lizzie moved on to the kitchen, with its brand-new cookstove, its stocked shelves. There was a table with four chairs; her father had built it himself, in his wood shop on the ranch.

In addition to the parlor and kitchen, there was a little bathroom with all the latest in plumbing. A bedroom stood on either side—the smaller one empty, the larger one furnished with a bureau and a wardrobe, donated by Lizzie's grandfather, but no bed.

"Where are we going to sleep?" Lizzie asked.

Morgan laughed and drew her into his arms. Kissed the tip of her nose. "I'm not planning on doing all that much sleeping," he said. "Not on our wedding night, at least."

Lizzie's cheeks burned with both anticipation and embarrassment. "Be practical," she said. "We need a bed. Shouldn't we order one at the mercantile?"

Morgan held her close, and then closer still. "Stop worrying," he said. "Things always turn out for the best, don't they? Look at Zebulon and Marietta—at John Brennan—and us."

Lizzie rested her forehead against Morgan's shoulder, content to be there, wrapped in his strong embrace. Things *had* turned out for the best—the Halifaxes were living happily on the Triple M, Ellen and Jack attending Chloe's school, rather than her own, because the ranch was a long way out of town. Whitley had written recently to say that he'd met the woman he wanted to marry; they'd met at a party following a polo match. Morgan's practice was thriving, though he earned next to nothing, and Lizzie loved teaching school.

"Do you ever think about Mr. Christian?" she asked.

Morgan stroked her hair. "Sometimes," he said. "Especially with Christmas coming on. Mostly, though, Lizzie McKettrick, I think about you."

She tilted her head back to look up into his face. "I love you, Dr. Morgan Shane," she said.

He kissed her, with a hungry tenderness, then forced himself to step back. They had been intimate, but never in the cottage. They were saving that.

"And I love you," he said, after catching his breath. "Does it bother you, Lizzie, to take my name? You won't be a McKettrick anymore, after we're married."

"I'll *always* be a McKettrick," Lizzie told him. "No matter what name I go by. I'll also be your wife, Morgan. I'll be Lizzie Shane."

He grinned, his hands resting lightly on her shoulders. His eyes glistened, and when he spoke, his voice came out sounding hoarse. "You're the best thing that ever happened to me," he said. "I never once thought—"

Lizzie stroked his cheek with gentle fingers still chilled from being outside in the snowy cold. "Hush," she told him. "Stop talking and kiss me again."

The main ranch house seemed about to burst at the corners, the morning of Christmas Eve, as Lizzie stood obediently on a milk stool in Angus and Concepcion's bedroom upstairs, feeling resplendent in her lacy wedding dress, while Lorelei and the aunts, Emmeline, Mandy and Chloe, pinned and stitched and chattered.

Katie, the child born late in life to Angus and Concepcion, now eleven-going-on-forty, as Lorelei liked to say, sat on the side of her parents' bed, watching the proceedings. With her dark hair and deep-blue eyes, Katie was exquisitely beautiful, although she hadn't realized it yet.

"When I get married," she said, her gaze sweeping over Lizzie's dress, "*I'm* not going to change my name. I'm still going to be Katie McKettrick, forever and ever, no matter what."

"You won't be getting married for a while yet," Chloe told her. Married to Lizzie's uncle Jeb, Chloe was a beauty herself, with copper-colored hair and bright, intelligent eyes. She taught all the children on and around the ranch in the little schoolhouse Jeb had built for her as a wedding present. "By then, you might have changed your mind about taking your husband's name."

Stubbornly, Katie folded her arms. "No, I won't," she said.

"You're just like your father," Concepcion told her daughter, entering the room and closing the door quickly behind her, so none of the men would get a glimpse of Lizzie in her dress. "Katie, Katie, quite contrary."

Lizzie smiled. "You'll make a very lovely bride," she told the little girl.

Katie beamed. "You look so pretty," she told Lizzie. "Like a fairy queen."

Lizzie thanked her, and the pinning and stitching went on. Finally, though, the sewing was done, and she was able to step behind the changing screen, shed the sumptuous dress and get back into her everyday garb. That day, it was a light-blue woolen frock with prim black piping and a high collar that tickled her under the chin.

Ducking around the screen again, she was surprised to see that though Concepcion, Lorelei and the aunts had gone, Katie remained.

Lizzie sat down on the bed beside her and draped an arm around Katie's shoulders. Although Katie was much younger, she was actually Lizzie's aunt, a half sister to Holt, Rafe, Jeb and Kade.

"All right," Lizzie said gently, "what's bothering you, Katie-did?"

Tears brimmed in Katie's eyes. "You're getting married," she said. "Everything is going to be different now."

"Not so different," Lizzie replied. "I'll still be your niece."

Katie giggled at that, and sniffled. "I missed you so much when you went away to San Francisco," she whispered.

Lizzie hugged her. "And I missed you. But I'm home now, and I'm staying."

"You're getting *married,*" Katie repeated insistently. "You're going to be Lizzie Shane, not Lizzie McKettrick. What if Morgan decides he doesn't like living in Indian Rock and takes you somewhere far away?"

"That isn't going to happen," Lizzie said.

"How can you be so sure? When a woman gets married, the man's the boss from then on. You have to do what he says."

Lizzie smiled. "Now, where would you have gotten such an idea, Katie McKettrick?" she teased. "Does your mama do what your papa tells her? Do any of your sisters-in-law take orders from your brothers?"

Katie brightened. "No," she said.

"Morgan and I have talked all this through, Katie. We're staying right in Indian Rock, for good. He'll do his doctoring, and I'll teach school."

"Will you have babies?"

The question made Lizzie squirm a little. She'd checked the calendar that morning, for a perfectly ordinary reason, and realized something important. "I certainly hope so," she said carefully.

Katie wrapped both arms around Lizzie and squeezed hard. "The little kids think St. Nicholas is coming on Christmas Eve," she confided. "But I'm big now, and I know it's Papa and Mama who fill my stocking and put presents under the tree."

"Do you, now?" Lizzie countered mysteriously, thinking of Nicholas Christian—Mr. Christmas, as the Halifax children had called him.

"You're all grown up," Katie said. "You don't believe in St. Nicholas."

"Maybe not precisely," Lizzie replied, "but I certainly believe in miracles."

"What kind of miracles?" Katie wanted to know. Young as she was, she had a tenaciously skeptical mind.

"I think angels visit earth, disguised as ordinary human beings, for one thing."

"Why would they do that?"

"Maybe to help us be strong and keep going when we're discouraged."

"Have you ever been discouraged, Lizzie?"

"Yes," Lizzie answered. "Last Christmas, when Morgan and I and all the rest of us were trapped aboard that train, up in the high country, I wondered if we'd make it home. I kept my chin up, but I was worried."

"You knew Papa and Holt and Rafe and Kade and Jeb would come get you," Katie insisted.

Lizzie nodded.

"Then why were you scared?"

"It was cold, and folks were sick and injured, and I was far away from all of you. There had been an avalanche, and one avalanche often leads to another."

"And an angel came? Did it have wings?"

Lizzie laughed. "No wings," she said. "Just a sample case and a flask of whiskey. He went out into the blizzard, though, and came back with a Christmas tree."

Katie wrinkled her nose, clearly disappointed. "That doesn't sound like any angel I've ever heard of," she replied. "They're supposed to fly, and have wings and halos—"

"Sometimes they have bowler hats and overcoats instead," Lizzie said. "I know I met an angel, Katie McKettrick, a real, live angel, and you're not going to change my mind."

"How did you *know?*" Katie wondered, intrigued in spite of herself. "That he was an angel, I mean?"

Lizzie glanced from side to side, even though they were alone in the room. "He disappeared," she said. "I was talking to him last year, around this time, in the schoolyard in town. I turned away for a moment, and when I looked back, he was gone."

Katie's wondrous eyes widened. "Are you joshing me, Lizzie?" she demanded. "I'm not a little kid anymore, you know."

Lizzie chuckled. "I'm telling you the truth," she said, holding up one hand, oath-giving style. "And you know what else? He didn't leave any footprints in the snow. Mine were there, and so were Morgan's, but it was as if Mr. Christmas hadn't been there at all."

Katie let out a long breath.

Lizzie gave her young aunt another squeeze. "The point of all this, Katie-did," she said, "is that it's important to believe in things, even when you're all grown up."

"I still don't believe in St. Nicholas," Katie said staunchly.

A knock sounded at the bedroom door, and Concepcion stuck her head in. "We're all leaving for town early," she announced. "Angus says the way this snow is coming down, we might be in for another Christmas blizzard."

Chapter Ten

The wind rattled the walls and windows of that sturdy little church, and as Holt McKettrick waited to walk his daughter up the aisle, following the Christmas Eve service, he thought about miracles. A year before, he'd come closer to losing Lizzie for good than he was willing to admit, even to himself. Now, here she stood, at his side, almost unbearably lovely in her wedding dress.

His little girl. About to be married.

Married.

She'd been twelve when she'd come to live with him—before that, he hadn't even known she existed. For a brief, poignant moment, he yearned for those lost years—Lizzie, learning to walk and talk. Wearing bows in her hair. Coming to him with skinned knees, disappointments and little-girl secrets.

But if there was one thing he'd learned in his life, it was that there was no sense in regretting the past. The *present,* that was what was important. It was all any of them really had.

The children in the congregation were restless, having sat through the service—it was Christmas Eve, after all—and the adults were eager. A low murmur rose from the crowd, and then a small voice rang out like a bell.

"Is it over yet?"

Doss, his and Lorelei's youngest.

The wedding guests laughed, and Holt joined in. Relaxed a little when his gaze connected with Lorelei's. She favored him with a smile and nodded slightly.

Holt nodded back. *I love you,* he told her silently.

And she nodded again.

Holt shifted his attention to the bridegroom.

The man standing up there at the altar, straight-backed and bright-eyed, was the *right* man for Lizzie, Holt was convinced of that. He suspected they'd jumped the gun a little, Lizzie and Morgan, and if Morgan hadn't been exactly who he was, Holt would have horsewhipped him for it.

They were young, as Lorelei had reminded him, when he'd told her he thought the bride and groom had been practicing up for the wedding night ahead of time, and they were in love.

He warmed at the memory of Lorelei's smile. "Remember how it was with us?" she'd asked. In truth, that part of their relationship hadn't changed. They had children and a home together now, so they couldn't be quite as spontaneous as they'd once been, but the passion between them was as fiery as ever.

The organist struck the first note of the wedding march.

"Ready?" Holt asked his daughter, his voice coming out gruff since there was a lump the size of Texas in his throat.

"Ready," Lizzie assured him gently, squeezing his arm. "I love you, Papa."

Tears scalded Holt's eyes. "I love you right back, Lizzie-bet," he replied.

And they started toward the front of the church, where Morgan and Preacher Reynolds waited. The crowd blurred around Holt, and he wondered if Lizzie sensed that they were stepping out of an old world and into a brand-new one. Things would be different after tonight.

She was so beautiful, Morgan thought, as he watched Lizzie gliding toward him on her father's arm, a vision in her spectacular home-sewn dress. There was love in every stitch and fold of that gown and in every tiny crystal bead glittering on the bodice. Though he wasn't a fanciful man, Morgan knew in that moment that one day he and Lizzie would have a daughter, and she, too, would wear this dress. He'd know how Holt felt, when that day came. At the moment, he could only guess.

Finally Lizzie stood beside him.

His head felt light, and he braced his knees. Damn, but he was lucky. Luckier than he'd ever dreamed he could be.

"Who giveth this woman in marriage?" the preacher asked, raising his voice to be heard over the blizzard raging outside.

"Lorelei and I do," Holt answered gravely. He kissed the top of Lizzie's head and went to sit beside Lorelei in the front pew, along with Angus and Concepcion.

Morgan smiled to himself. Earlier in the evening, Angus had informed him, in no uncertain terms, that if he ever did anything to hurt Lizzie, he'd get a hiding for it.

The holy words were said, the vows exchanged.

And then the preacher pronounced Lizzie and Morgan man and wife.

"You may kiss the bride," Reynolds said.

His hands shaking a little—the hands that were so steady holding a scalpel or binding a wound—Morgan raised Lizzie's veil and gazed down into her upturned face, wonderstruck. She glowed, as though a light were burning inside her.

He kissed her, not hungrily, as he would later that night, when they were alone in the cottage, but reverently. A sacred charge passed between them, as though they had not only been joined on earth, but in heaven, too, and for all of time and eternity.

The organ thundered again, a joyous, triumphant sound, bouncing off the walls of that frontier church, and again a child's voice piped above the joyous chaos.

"It's over!"

Morgan laughed along with everybody else, but he was thinking, *It isn't over. Oh, no. This is only the start.*

The reception was held in the lobby of the Arizona Hotel, where a giant Christmas tree loomed over the proceedings, glittering with tinsel and blown-glass balls, presents piled high beneath it. Knowing the family wouldn't be able to get back to the ranch after the wedding, because of the storm, Lizzie's grandfather had had everything loaded onto hay sleds and brought to town. Most of the McKettricks would be staying at the hotel, while the overflow spent the night with the Thaddingses.

Lizzie, dazed with happiness, ate cake and posed for the photographer, with Morgan beside her. There were piles of wedding gifts: homemade quilts, preserves, embroidered dish towels and pillowcases. She was hugged, kissed, congratulated and teased.

A band played, and she danced with her father first, then her grandfather, then each of her uncles in turn. By the time Morgan claimed *his* dance, Lizzie was winded.

When the time finally came for her and Morgan to take their leave, Lizzie was both relieved and quivery with nervous anticipation. She was Morgan's *wife,* now. And she had a gift for him that couldn't be wrapped in pretty paper and tied with a shimmery ribbon.

How would he respond when she told him?

A horse-drawn sleigh awaited the bride and groom in the snowy street outside. Lizzie left her veil in Lorelei's care, and they hastened toward the sleigh, Morgan bundling Lizzie quickly in thick blankets before huddling in beside her. Looking through the blinding flurries of white, she saw a figure hunched at the reins and wondered which of her uncles was driving.

The sleigh carried them swiftly through the night.

Lamps burned in the cottage windows when they arrived, glowing golden through the storm.

Morgan helped Lizzie down from the sleigh, swept her up into his arms, and carried her up the path to the front door. Looking back over her new husband's shoulder, Lizzie caught the briefest glimpse of the driver as he lifted his hat, and recognized Mr. Christmas. She started to call out to him, but the blizzard intensified and horse, sleigh and driver disappeared in a great, glittering swirl of snow.

And then they were inside, over the threshold.

Someone had decorated a small Christmas tree, and placed it on a table in front of the window. Lizzie nearly knocked it over, rushing to look outside, hoping to see her unlikely angel again.

The wind had stopped, and the snow fell softly now, slowly, big, fluffy flakes of it, blanketing the street in peace.

"Lizzie, what is it?" Morgan asked, standing behind her, wrapping his arms around her waist and drawing her back against him.

"I thought I saw—"

"What?"

She sighed, turned to Morgan, smiled up at him. "I thought I saw an angel," she said.

Morgan smiled, kissed her forehead. "It's Christmas Eve. There might be an angel or two around."

Lizzie swallowed, thinking that if she loved this man even a little bit more, she'd burst with the pure, elemental force of it. She paused, smiled. "I have a Christmas gift for you, Morgan," she told him, very quietly.

He glanced down at the packages under the little tree, raised an eyebrow in question.

She took his hand, pressed it lightly to her lower abdomen. "A baby," she said. "We're going to have a baby."

Morgan's face was a study in startled delight. "When, Lizzie?"

"July, I think," she replied, feeling shy. And much relieved. A part of her hadn't been sure Morgan would be pleased, since they were so newly married and had yet to establish a home together.

Gently, Morgan untied the laces of her cloak, slid it off her shoulders, laid it aside. "July," he repeated.

"There'll be some gossip," she warned. "I'm the schoolmarm, after all."

Morgan chuckled, his eyes alight with love. "You know what they say. The first baby can come anytime, the rest take nine months."

Lizzie was too happy to worry about gossip. She wasn't the first pregnant bride in Indian Rock, or in the McKettrick family, and she wouldn't be the last. "You're really glad, then?" She had to ask. "You don't wish we'd had more time?"

"I wouldn't change anything, Lizzie. Not anything at all."

She sniffled. "I love you so much it scares me, Dr. Morgan Shane."

He kissed her, lightly, the way he'd done in front of the altar earlier that night, when the preacher pronounced them man and wife. "And I love you, Mrs. Shane."

She laughed, and they drew apart, and Lizzie glanced at the little tree and the packages beneath it. "Did you do this?" she asked.

Morgan shook his head. "I thought you did," he replied.

"It must have been Lorelei, or the aunts," Lizzie said, pleasantly puzzled. She picked up one of the packages and recognized her stepmother's handwriting. "To Morgan," the tag read. "Open it," she urged.

Morgan's expression showed clearly that he had other things in mind than opening Christmas presents, but he took the parcel and unwrapped it just the same. Inside was an exquisitely made toy locomotive, of shining black metal—a reminder of how he and Lizzie had met.

He smiled, admiring it. "Open yours," he said.

Lizzie reached for the second parcel, gently tore away the ribbon and brightly colored paper. Lorelei had given her a baby's christening gown, frothy with lace, and a tiny bonnet to match.

"They *knew,*" she marveled.

Morgan's grin was mischievous. "Maybe we were too obvious," he said.

Lizzie's cheeks warmed.

Morgan laughed and curved a finger under her chin. "Lizzie," he said, "Holt and Lorelei aren't exactly doddering old folks. They're in love, too, remember?"

She smiled. Nodded. "I'd like to change out of this dress," she said.

Morgan's eyes smoldered. "You do that," he replied gruffly. "I'll build up the fire a little."

Lizzie nodded and headed for the bedroom, stopping on the threshold to gasp. "Morgan!" she called.

He joined her.

A beautiful bed stood in the place that had been so noticeably vacant before, the headboard intricately carved with the image of a great, leafy oak, spreading its branches alongside a flowing creek. Birds soared against a cloud-strewn sky, and both their names had been carved into the trunk of the tree, inside a heart. Lizzie + Morgan.

Lizzie drew in her breath. This was her father's wedding gift, to her and to Morgan. It was more than a piece of furniture, more than an heirloom that would be passed down for generations. It was his *blessing,* on them and on their marriage.

"Lizzie McKettrick Shane," Morgan said, leaning to kiss the side of her neck, "you come from quite a family."

She nodded, moved closer to the bed, stroked the fine woodwork with the tips of her fingers, marveling at the time, thought and love that had gone into such a creation. "And now you're part of it," she told Morgan. "You and our baby and all the other babies that will come along later."

Morgan lingered in the doorway, framed there, looking so handsome in his new suit, specially bought for the wedding, that Lizzie etched the moment into her memory, to keep forever. *Her husband.* Even when she was an old, old lady, creaky-boned and wrinkled, she knew she would recall every detail of the way he looked that night.

"I'll see to the fire," he said, after a long, long time.

Lizzie nodded, shyly now. Waited until Morgan

had stepped away from the door before taking a lacy nightgown from the trunk containing her trousseau and changing into it. She folded her wedding gown carefully, placed it in a box set aside for the purpose. She took down her hair and brushed it in front of the vanity mirror until it shone.

Morgan had never seen her with her hair down.

Warmth filled the cottage and, one by one, the lamps in the parlor went out. Lizzie waited, her heart racing a little.

Morgan filled the bedroom doorway again, a man-shaped shadow, rimmed in faint, wintry light. The sweet silence of the snow outside seemed to muffle all sound. They might have been alone in the world that Christmas Eve, she and Morgan, two wanderers who'd somehow found their way to each other after long and difficult journeys.

Morgan whispered her name, came toward her.

She slipped into his arms.

They'd looked forward to making love on their wedding night, both of them. Now, by tacit agreement, they waited, savoring every nuance of being together.

Morgan threaded his hands through Lizzie's hair.

She felt beautiful.

"To think," Morgan said quietly, "that I almost didn't get on that train last Christmas."

"Don't think," Lizzie teased. He'd said the same thing to her, once, while they were stranded on the mountainside.

He chuckled, and kissed her with restrained passion. Eagerness and wanting sang through Lizzie, but she was willing to wait. There was no hurry: she and Morgan were married now, after all. They would make love countless times in the days, weeks, months and years ahead.

They'd already conceived a child, and Lizzie knew something of the pleasures awaiting her, but tonight was special. It was their first time as husband and wife.

Her breath caught, and her heartbeat quickened as Morgan caressed her, touching her lightly in all the places she loved to be touched, all the places she *needed* to be touched.

She gave herself up to him, completely, joyously, with little gasps and sighs as he pleasured her, slowly. Ever so slowly, and with such expertise that Lizzie wished that night would never end.

She was transported, in the bed with the tree carved into the headboard. She died there, and was reborn, a new woman, even stronger than before. She gasped and whimpered and sobbed out Morgan's name, clinging to him with everything she had, riding wave after wave of sacred satisfaction.

Hours passed before they slept, sated and spent, arms and legs entwined.

Lizzie awakened first, to the cold, snowy light of a clear Christmas morning. The fire had gone out during the night, but she was warm, through and through, snuggled close to Morgan under a heavy layer of quilts.

He stirred beside her, opened his eyes. "I'd better get the fire going," he said, his voice sleepy.

"Not yet," Lizzie whispered, burrowing closer to him.

"We'll freeze," he said.

Lizzie laughed and shook her head. "I don't think so," she answered, nibbling mischievously at his neck.

He rolled on top of her, his elbows pressed into the mattress on either side. "Have I married a hussy?" he asked.

"Most definitely," Lizzie answered, beaming. "And you thought I was only a schoolmarm."

Morgan laughed, and the sound was beautiful to Lizzie, and in the distance the church bells pealed, ringing in Christmas.

Center Point Publishing
600 Brooks Road • PO Box 1
Thorndike ME 04986-0001 USA

(207) 568-3717

US & Canada:
1 800 929-9108
www.centerpointlargeprint.com